Biblioasis International Translation Series
General Editor: Stephen Henighan

OSCAR

MAURICIO

Segura

OSCAR

**TRANSLATED
FROM THE FRENCH
BY DONALD WINKLER**

BIBLIOASIS
WINDSOR, ONTARIO

For the poem cited on page 140, see Derek Walcott, "Love After Love," *Collected Poems, 1948-1984*, Farrar, Straus and Giroux, 1986, p. 328.

FIRST EDITION

Library and Archives Canada Cataloguing in Publication

Segura, Mauricio, 1969-
[Oscar. English]
        Oscar / Mauricio Segura ; [translated by] Donald Winkler.

(Biblioasis international translation series ; 23)
Translation of: Oscar.
Issued in print and electronic formats.
ISBN 978-1-77196-225-4 (softcover).--ISBN 978-1-77196-226-1 (ebook)

        I. Winkler, Donald, translator II. Title. III. Title: Oscar. English
V. Series: Biblioasis international translation series ; 23

PS8587.E384O8213 2018   C843'.54   C2017-907311-7
                                                 C2017-907312-5

Edited by Stephen Henighan and Daniel Wells
Copy-edited by Jessica Faulds
Cover designed by Gordon Robertson
Typeset by Chris Andrechek

Published with the generous assistance of the Canada Council for the Arts, which last year invested $153 million to bring the arts to Canadians throughout the country. Biblioasis also acknowledges the support of the Ontario Arts Council (OAC), an agency of the Government of Ontario, which last year funded 1,709 individual artists and 1,078 organizations in 204 communities across Ontario, for a total of $52.1 million, and the contribution of the Government of Ontario through the Ontario Book Publishing Tax Credit and the Ontario Media Development Corporation. Biblioasis also acknowledges the financial support of the Government of Canada through the National Translation Program for Book Publishing, an initiative of the *Roadmap for Canada's Official Languages 2013–2018: Education, Immigration, Communities*, for our translation activities.

PRINTED AND BOUND IN CANADA

For Thomas

1

Just before meeting the devil in person, that fateful morning with its ashen sky, Oscar was gazing down at his reflection in the canal's oily waters with the firm intention of putting an end to his days. There were two or three people—at a factory window, on the footbridge over a lock, atop the church steeple next to his parents' house—who might have recognized from afar his imposing silhouette through the layers of stagnant fog that strangely, that day, no wind had come to disturb. Most of the inhabitants of Little Burgundy knew that in recent months, O.P., as everyone affectionately called him, had been in a bad way, as there'd been little sign of him in the jazz bars. Some said that he'd been trying to forget himself by working as a docker in the port, others that he was wandering about like a lost soul. But no one suspected that his despair ran so deep. So much so that when the news got around that he'd tried to take his own life, his pockets full of stones, and had been saved *in extremis* by a mysterious stranger, everyone was taken unawares, because up to that point his virtuosity at the keyboard had seemed proof positive of his character's innate buoyancy. Had not his boogie-woogies cheered up terminally ill patients? Had not his ballads softened the hearts of many girls being wooed by young men who were at a loss for seductive guile?

Speculation surrounding his suicide attempt soon grew to the point where it assumed the fantastical and disquieting guise of tavern banter. His admirers cited an instance, imagined from beginning to end, of malicious gossip being circulated by those who were jealous of him. His detractors, for their part, speculated on the causes for the affliction that was weighing him down. Was he having trouble with his young wife? With his father? The owner of the Twilight Station Bar, where he regularly performed? Had he forgotten that after the twelfth stroke of midnight you had to take the shortest route home if you didn't want the spirits to make you forget where you lived? Had he met a solitary crow perched on one of the three scrawny maples still left standing near the canal? Others wondered aloud what was in his mind as, despondent, he walked the length of the canal's polluted waters. Had he, as it had been known to happen, seen his life pass before him in a flash?

But no! cried old Jackson, who since the beginning of time had been rocking herself back and forth in front of her humble abode, her face tilted to the sun as if the trade wind itself were at play in her dry, witchy hair. That's not the way we do things! We don't look to the past when we're about to give up the ghost; what we conjure in our heads is a paradise where we're going to put down stakes, with a beach, coconut trees, a horizon that goes on and on, and—*bloodseed!*—enough rum to last, God help us, for all eternity! But no one's perfect, and on this particular occasion everything would suggest that old Jackson was wrong, since if you can take Oscar at his word, there was a wrathful gale that rose up in his mind on that day, to sweep away telephone poles as if they were matchsticks, to rip up newly paved roads, to send flying through the air the factory CEOs' state-of-the-art streamlined automobiles, and to hurl O.P. himself back several decades, to his father's first days in Montreal.

It was already the age of steel. The quilts of melon and turnip fields were no more than a glowing memory in the minds of the neighbourhood's elders. Like a deep seam, the canal had been dug for some time, while the two rail lines, like zippers, marked off the neighbourhood to the north and the south. Dozens of factories lined the streets, their chimneys exhaling, without ever pausing for breath, smoke of all conceivable shades of grey. That smoke coated the trees with soot from head to foot and darkened the windows of the trams passing by, first hauled by horses, then powered by the hidden magic of electricity; it perturbed the passengers with their noses pressed to the windows and masked the tired faces of the workers who, with their checkered caps and their lunch tucked under their arms, stepped resignedly over the thresholds ushering them into confines where the piston held sway. For some, this gloom was the price to pay for everyone being able to earn his daily bread by the sweat of his brow; for others, those factories were leading humanity to its ruin. It was in this climate of hope tinged with apocalyptic apprehension that the first members of the community arrived on the scene.

Oscar never needed much coaxing to talk about that period in his father's life. The fact is that as soon as Josué learned that he'd landed in a city that was also an island, he decided to make it his home, for certainly among islanders they'd be surrounded by soul mates. In the very first week, since he had a passion for stars, he tried his luck as professor of astronomy at the university, even though he'd never completed his fourth year of schooling. It appears that on the high seas, when he was leading the harsh life of a seaman, and while after dark his companions vied with each other as to who could get drunk the fastest, he played the organ—an old portable set into mahogany—or scanned the heavens with the help of a telescope. He'd come across those objects, both replete with an instruction manual, as he wandered the boat's hold one night, while the ship's freebooter captain snored away, an empty bottle of rum clutched to his breast. While the others partied on the bridge, he practised his scales and arpeggios on the forecastle in the open air; then, as his companions were dropping like flies, having spewed out their innards, he studied the celestial bodies, one eye to the telescope's eyepiece, like a child peering through a keyhole.

Josué wanted to know music well enough to learn by ear the airs he'd grown up with, airs that beguiled some of the sailors to the point of luring them into the arms of nostalgia, and then those of Morpheus. As for astronomy, despite the constant roiling of the seas that shunted the telescope from left to right, from right to left, he made great progress in his first observations: within a few weeks, the moon, the sun, the stars, and the principal constellations became for him familiar stopping places, just like a grocery store or a bakery for any other mortal. Yet it was the Milky Way that enthralled him; recalling a passage in his astronomy manual that dealt with the Andromeda Galaxy and its spiral shape, he saw, after skilful calculations, and thanks in part to the salt sea odour, that our galaxy too is intriguingly womb-like, its libidinous curves in constant flux, and that is why, to make things clear, he baptised it the Way of Desire.

And so, a few days after his arrival in the city where the great O.P. was to be born, Josué visited, one by one, all its universities. Wearing a brand new pale-grey suit—he had sunk all their savings into it, to the despair of Davina, his wife—with a yellow hibiscus from his native island, miraculously conserved, in his button hole, he braved the precincts of those venerable institutions, introducing himself in a resonant voice as the most reliable authority on the Way of Desire, given his revolutionary discovery and his seven-thousand-three-hundred-and-fifty-four hours of direct observation. As soon as his voice began to echo through the entrance halls, security guards materialized without fail from who knows where and barred his way. Sometimes, even, his evictors—who certainly knew nothing of the call of the stars—took him by the arms and, with Josué's feet pedalling in the void a metre off the ground, escorted him to the exit and sent him tumbling down the stairs like a ball of wool. As he got to his feet and brushed himself off, trying as he might to make sense of it all, he couldn't understand why he, a light unto the peoples, who had withstood so many winds and storms all for the good of humanity, was being treated in such a way. Never, even in his few disconsolate moments, would he have imagined deserving such a rebuff.

After this setback, when he was offered, like other West Indians, a job as porter with the Canadian National Railways, he accepted, but with a plan in mind. He left on Sunday nights—with under his arm a dish prepared by his wife, into which she took care to deposit a large red pepper to ward off the evil spirits which, everyone knows, circulate freely on overnight trains—crossed the country from east to west, catering to the comfort of the passengers, then took the same route back in the opposite direction. During the four hours the porters were allotted for sleep, he hoisted himself onto the rail-car's roof along with his portable telescope and, ringed round by the prairies' purple sky, despite the lurchings of the train, gave himself over heart and soul to his grapplings with the mysteries of the universe that were complicating his life. Despite his miserable salary and the harsh treatment he received from his superiors, he'd found a way to follow his dream. When Josué arrived back home, Davina asked him why he seemed so bone-tired, but his only reply was to say I'll tell you one day, while turning his back to drift off, muttering a few mathematical formulas, his forehead still glued to a telescope which itself, no doubt, was in need of recuperation.

It was about this same time that Brad, O.P.'s pint-sized older brother, began to play technically perfect scales on his father's portable organ, even though no one had given him any lessons. After a few weeks he became bored with the instrument's two octaves, and his fingers began to work away at the empty air to the left and right of the keyboard, producing very high and very low notes that only he could hear. Fate's own fickle finger then awarded him what most in the world he dreamed might come to pass: a francophone neighbour, moved by the child's passion for music, sold them for a pittance an old piano on which her late husband used to tinkle away Sunday afternoons. From then on Brad played without stopping, bewitched by the instrument: in the morning after breakfast; in his school's music room; at night, after doing his homework, drawing crowds to the stone staircase outside their house, where young people danced in the summer and jumped up and down and blew on their hands in winter, enthralled by those swelling notes that evoked dance floors swept by gowns with beaded hems. Sundays, he sat at the church organ and with his rendering of the gospels had hot tears, unstoppable, coursing down the cheeks of the faithful. He practised his scales to such a late hour that his parents ordered his older sister, Prudence, to force him into bed.

Oscar's birth was greeted with about as much enthusiasm as the knife-grinder's sporadic appearances, because in the midst of life's mundane tasks there was not much time left for outpourings of emotion. He was born, one might say, without fanfare, though not entirely, because the trumpet salvaged from a pile of refuse in the park, which had long sat on the upright in the living room because no family member wanted to play it, was thrust into his hands once he'd turned his back on the piano. For him the piano was Brad's alone.

After Oscar spent two days trying to get a sound out of the horn, the novelty wore off, and it was restored to its former spot, and its patina of dust. Had you followed him through the byways of the neighbourhood, it would have been hard to imagine that deep down in Oscar there was hidden a great artist. He swept past the neighbours—old men in rocking chairs, drunkards in heated dialogue with their demons, vegetable hawkers with nasal voices, paranoid bookmakers, sun-struck banjo players, and, above all, crowds and crowds of children—a horseshoe in his hand, or perhaps a comics page ripped from a newspaper stolen from a delivery boy. Never mind if his parents urged him to spend more time on his homework, he always managed to slip away to the street, his true kingdom. There everyone knew him, and he knew everyone, to the point where, decades later, it surprised no one that the neighbourhood's hustle and bustle inspired some of his most beautiful compositions.

Friday night, in summer, a kite rose into the sky, gaily swaying, as if to thumb its nose at the law of gravity. From behind a wooden fence that was threatening to collapse, O.P. appeared and disappeared, taller and chubbier than the other children. Fascinated, he followed with his eyes the ripplings of the kite's sail, its cheeky wiggling, its suicidal dives, until he heard a plaintive whistle tearing through the night, eclipsing both the ambient noise and his own good humour. His singling out of the train's wail, alike in pitch to what he'd been able to coax from the trumpet, is a first indication that there was indeed a musician lurking somewhere inside him. It was this keening that warned him of his father's imminent return. While the iron monster burrowed through the darkness, sucking up everything in its path and transforming it as it went into a din interrupted by loud sighs, O.P., before moving on, handed the kite-steering stick to his neighbour, and it was not rare to see it slip from his friend's grip and drift off slowly into the night's vastness, like a man falling backwards over a precipice.

He dashed diagonally across two or three streets, chased away some stray dogs sniffing at his behind, waved to people he knew, and, hearing the cascade of notes his brother was loosing from the family piano, which always reminded him of a drunken bum tumbling downstairs in a bar, he entered his house, sliding past the music lovers huddled in front of the door. He stopped at the edge of the living room to watch Brad's fingers race across the keyboard and he was filled with joy, but also a curious melancholy. What exactly was he feeling? Both a deep admiration for his brother and already a faint stirring of envy? The pride of belonging to the same family as someone remarkable, along with the chagrin of knowing that he was not one of the elect? Reluctantly, he grabbed the trumpet and took it to his room, hurriedly applying himself to the exercises his father had assigned him.

As soon as he arrived home, Josué took off his porter's uniform, the jacket with multiple buttons that was tight around his neck, and the cap he abhorred, and shut himself away to take a warm bath. He then sank down into the living room armchair, where no one else dared rest his backside during his absence, to listen to O.P. on the trumpet. But as soon as he heard the discordant moan his son extracted from the instrument, he shook his head, his eyes dimmed with disappointment, and as the doors to all the rooms in the house shut one by one as if there were spirits at work, he reminded Oscar, just as his own father had once admonished him, that idle souls never get what they want, while the souls of the diligent are always rewarded.

In less time than it takes to play a game of dominos, the neighbourhood was swarming with members of his community and its streets were redolent with jerk chicken and plantain, whose aromas overpowered the reek from the factories and excited the taste buds of all who passed that way. One summer, something strange occurred that attracted the attention of the keenest minds in Montreal. The sun, it appeared, was setting almost an hour and a half later in the neighbourhood than anywhere else in the city. This remarkable observation was succeeded by another the following autumn: the neighbourhood's maple leaves changed colour three weeks later than those in the other boroughs. It was then noted that that winter was giving up the ghost earlier than usual; the snow melted in the streets like sugar in coffee, even as blizzards blew in the surrounding districts. Finally, when spring showed its first signs of life, the tulips rose from the ground a month before those in the flower beds in the centre of town. *Bloodseed*, what did it all mean?

On a sunny Saturday afternoon, while Brad was rehearsing a ragtime that was all the rage on the radio, O.P. went out looking for his friends in the park, and his eyes were greeted by a rainbow so vivid that it seemed as if he could touch it. Dazzled by the unreal colours, O.P. suddenly stopped where he was, because he could have sworn that he saw rain in the distance, over the business district. So as to be clear in his own mind, undistracted by his friends' intrusive questions, O.P. made his way to the edge of Little Burgundy and found that he was right: rain was pouring down on the other side of the street, while where he stood, not a drop was dampening the sidewalk. For weeks he turned the question over in his mind, but he could not solve the mystery: why was his neighbourhood being blessed with a milder climate than others?

After several days of surveillance, perched all alone up in the park's bleachers while his friends begged him to stop brooding and to come and play, he had a revelation. A few moments before, just as Brad was coming out of the house to take up his position as shortstop in the middle of the road, a mass of dark clouds had rolled across the sky, provoking a sudden violent rainstorm shortly thereafter. Later that afternoon, as Oscar was looking on, Brad slammed the door of the family home to head down, now, to the port, where he was working on the docks to earn some extra money. Once again, the cloudless sky covered over in an instant, and a torrential rain beat down on the neighbourhood. *Bloodseed*, murmured O.P., his eyes shining: as soon as Brad stopped playing his transcendent music, the bad weather returned. Oscar climbed the steps leading to his house four at a time, and it's said that in the middle of the living room, with great solemnity, he revealed his discovery to his father and his brothers and sisters. When he had finished speaking, the family members just looked at him, with knowing smiles on their faces. Davina, his mother, who had heard everything, stalked into the living room, wiping her hands on the apron she never removed. With a fierce scowl she sucked air in through her teeth, just like the good-for-nothings who hung out at the end of the block. Are you some kind of birdbrain, or what? she asked him. Is this some kind of joke? It's just come to you now that the All Powerful has blessed Brad with a gift that brings light into our lives? As Oscar looked on stupefied, she uttered a string of words under her breath that he had only heard before from the mobsters cruising the neighbourhood. Then she went back to her stove. But that sentence—Are you some kind of birdbrain, or what?—came back to him without fail for the rest of his life in times of crisis, suggesting that even as he stepped up to the canal, determined to end it all, they were echoing in his head.

From the very outset, O.P. had feared his mother, who never left the kitchen other than to go to bed and dream of dishes she would prepare the next day. The only exception was on the last Thursday of the month when, with a shawl over her head that she'd brought with her from the island of her birth, she went to deposit her husband's paycheque at the neighbourhood bank. She was not always easy to fathom, she had her quirks: she never sat down just after someone had freed up a chair, it's well known that brings bad luck; when she pulled hair off her comb, she was careful to toss it into the garbage can right away so that birds wouldn't get hold of the tufts to make a nest—everyone knows that can give you terrible headaches. Countless times since his early childhood, O.P. had seen his mother's unlikely predictions come to pass, and he had total faith in everything she said.

That is why the whole family—except for Josué, who at that very moment, in a first-class car, was handing an extra cushion to a disdainful, pouting lady—drank in every word when she came home one Thursday afternoon, awash in tears. This woman, who was as formidable as the local toughs, who virtually never cried, not even when she hurt herself, was visibly shaken. She began by telling them, short of breath, her lips trembling, that she had accidentally dropped her purse at the bank. As her comb bounced off the ground and her coins rolled to the four corners of the vast hall with its marble floors, another lady—just as absentminded, you'd have to believe—also lost hold of her purse. If Davina had been the only one to make that blunder, she and only she would have been hit with a stretch of bad luck, and things would have ended there, she said, rubbing her hands together as if trying to rid herself of a mote of imaginary dust. But two purses on the ground, did they see what that meant? While the cashiers, handymen, and security guards were down on their hands and knees, she could only foresee the disastrous impact this would have on the world, and Montreal in particular. A death-like silence descended on the room; then, to everyone's astonishment, she wiped the tears from her cheeks with a quick gesture, turned on her heels, and went back to her stove.

When Josué came home a few days later, the children told him about Davina's misadventure at the bank. Josué straight away burst into the kitchen to demand that his wife tell him in detail what that "disastrous impact" was to be. But she, as if fearing the power her predictions had of coming true, chose to remain silent. Josué spent the entire day pleading with her to tell the family something so it could prepare itself for the calamities that were to befall them, but Davina went about her business as if she were deaf. Josué, for his part, decided to answer in kind: when she tried to talk to him about the children's neglected geometry assignments, or about the men's shirts that he'd been offered by the church, he also behaved as though he'd lost his hearing.

One night, according to Oscar's sisters, as Josué was listening to the news on the radio, his wife appeared at the door to the living room. In a sepulchral voice, she predicted that the world was to face terrible suffering, that fathers of families would lose their jobs, that women of good character would be forced to debase themselves in order to survive. She saw them all, she said, as if they were filing past her in the living room, both working men and men of privilege sinking into despair, some going so far as to hang themselves or cut their throats. Josué remained silent, petrified. The children, hearing these horrifying prophecies, clung to their mother's skirts. Reluctantly, Josué agreed to Brad's proposal that the older offspring be allowed to work as long as the hard times lasted. Davina, who was not done with her revelations, confessed that she had one last prediction to share, the most terrible of all. If she could trust the abundance of porcelain roses and balsamic perfumes that appeared in her dreams, one of their own would depart this life, probably one of the children. Josué went to her and seized her hands, imploring her to find out the cause for this loss that was bearing down on them. For once she obeyed, rolling her eyes upwards and chanting invocations, calling on the spirits to come to her aid, but as she was only able, apparently, to make out a single picture in her head, she could just say over and over again: The child will die from asphyxiation, as though drowned at the bottom of a lake.

The days that followed were filled with dread. Everything was viewed in a dismal light: a new acquaintance of one of the boys' was regarded as suspicious, a new pastime of one of the girls' looked as lethal as walking on the guardrail of a bridge. When one of the children went for a walk downtown, Josué asked another to follow in case something happened and he needed help, you couldn't be too careful. If he had a day off during the week, Josué spied on his children in the schoolyard, monitoring in secret the girls' feats with the skipping rope and the boys' dexterity with their marbles.

To help out, and because it paid better than his little jobs at the dock, Brad performed as a pianist just a few steps from the house, in a jazz bar whose owners came from the same island as his parents. For a while now the neighbourhood had been alive with these places, from which there escaped, along with the inevitable neon glow, bits of heartfelt solos along with bursts of applause, like a cricket concert on a summer night. It was for the most part West Indian musicians who played there, the same ones who, oddly, were denied access to the other bars in the city because, it was claimed, they might make some clients uneasy, sensitive souls unaccustomed to island behaviour, which was seen as being "too spontaneous." Strangely, those same sensitive souls were not at all troubled when members of the community cleaned their houses or their train compartments on the way out of town. Still, you could find in the local bars West Indian musicians from the United States who, if you could trust what they said, were beleaguered even more by those sensitive souls threatening to faint away every time they spotted an islander in one of their watering holes. What is more, there was something strange going on south of the border. Preachers, made uncomfortable by the growing proportion of congregants that enjoyed the odd tipple, had started banning alcohol, persuaded that it was Satan's elixir, put there to pave the way for His seizing power. After having convinced the politicians of the urgent need to outlaw the production of this satanic poison, they now dreamed of shutting down all drinking establishments, thereby purging towns and villages of every last drop of alcohol. That is why, when the Americans wanted to forget their cares over a glass, their only option was to cross the border and spend an evening or weekend in a nearby city, most often Montreal.

In the neighbourhood, opinions were divided on those places. Some vaunted the creativity and determination of the musicians who played with their guts, hearts, and heads. This jazz, it was argued, wasn't just music for shaking your bones, but was also for elevating your spirit. Had one forgotten the cricket song of which the elders spoke, which calmed them on their native island after a long day slaving in the cotton fields? Well, these improvisations were the same thing, *bredda*. Others, like Josué, saw them on the contrary as dens of iniquity, where the community's bad apples could find an outlet for their morbid impulses. It was even said that all they did was to regale a rabble of hot-tempered bandits, devious pimps, and prostitutes, proving, as if proof were needed, that woman is a cat, and man a zombie.

Josué allowed his son to work there, on the condition that he would go with him to the bar's door and wait for him, studying one of his astronomy manuals. When O.P. and his friends passed the bar where Brad was playing, they tiptoed to the steamed-up window as if a fabulous dream were unfolding beyond it, and they scanned, wide-eyed, the feverish activity on the inside: women sat on men's knees; cigarette girls zigzagged between round tables, showing off their net stockings; jazzmen sporting gangster hats came and went and, when they emerged for a breath of fresh air, lifted their sunglasses to wink at them; men in three-piece suits arrived in shiny cars; and always and forever, gang bosses with angular faces stamped their feet, cigarettes in the corners of their mouths, making themselves scarce as soon as the police came by doing their rounds. It all ended abruptly for O.P. and his friends when the doorman burst onto the sidewalk and ordered them to get lost. Once in the park's sports stands, his friends talked about envying Brad, who was earning pocket money, had risen to be a local celebrity, and could now make conquests among the prettiest girls in the neighbourhood. Oscar shrugged his shoulders and said he was happy for his brother but that that was no life for him, practising scales for hours at a time, thank you very much.

As Brad was now performing at night, the sun refused to set, disturbing the sleep of many of the neighbourhood's residents. To combat their insomnia, the men began asking their wives to prepare them a glass of hot milk mixed with a spoonful of lime-blossom honey and a little orange-flower water, picked up at a West Indian grocery store that had just opened in the neighbourhood. When the jazzmen came out of the bars and were greeted by this strange nocturnal sun, they gazed up at the sky, and those with wristwatches stared at them, grumbling that they had to get them repaired, while those who had none decided that while they were playing, they'd lost track of time. The women were ecstatic: the fruits and vegetables in their gardens grew as rapidly as the calabash trees on the islands their parents had left behind.

Meanwhile, Davina's baleful prophecies were being fulfilled one by one. It seemed that the evil had its source in the highest spheres, among those most favoured, bankers in particular. A strange vermin, ravenous and insatiable, which attacked both wood and stone, was patiently eating away at the structures of their businesses, until they collapsed like houses of cards. What is more, it turned out that by sitting all day long on their behinds counting banknotes behind iron grills, these wealthy individuals had themselves been stung by the vermin, which had somehow managed to migrate from the employees' chairs up to their buttocks. These individuals began to lend money impulsively, their shoulders rocked by an infectious hilarity, to the point where they engineered the failure of their own institutions. Doctors put these curious patients under observation for days at a time, strapped into straitjackets to stop them from making more loans, and, after careful deliberation, concluded that they had contracted the virus of magnanimity. All of Montreal suffered the consequences: factories closed, businessmen were condemned to live in dire poverty, and thousands and thousands of workers, often after an enormous binge, ended their lives, just as Davina had foreseen.

No one paid much attention on the rainy afternoon when Brad came home with a cough, given that it was the magnanimity virus that was on everyone's mind. And not for nothing, because day and night, the radio spoke only of the industrialists' despair, the workers' joblessness, and the helplessness of the authorities. It was only when he began to spit copiously, to visibly lose weight, and to be afflicted with night sweats that his mother had him drink water with lemon juice, honey, and a pinch of cayenne. That drink was administered to him every half hour, to the point where he spent half his time crouched over the chamber pot. For a few days it calmed the tickling in his throat, and it seemed that the problem had been solved. But a week later his cough was back in force. One night, while Brad was coughing hard enough to break the hearts of those dear to him who were gathered round, Josué remembered having seen some musicians from Brad's group coughing, one harder than the other, on the way out of the bar one night, and he slapped his forehead: he'd been wrong to attribute that to too much smoking. Certain that he'd discovered the cause for the sickness eating away at his son, he told his wife about his discovery, while reconfirming his loathing for those places of debauchery. Davina placed the back of her hand against her son's mouth while closely monitoring his response before concluding: He's struggling to breathe, it's as if he were underwater. Then she froze, realizing what she'd said, remembering her terrible prophecy that one of her children would perish as if at the bottom of a lake. She understood that the die had been cast, that the All Powerful had already determined the fate of her child prodigy.

It's said that over the following days Brad lost so much weight that he seemed to shrink, even to appear younger. He seemed to want to go back in time, because he no longer behaved like an adolescent, but like a child who, between two fits of coughing, pointed to an object such as a vase or a mirror, asking what it was, and inquiring about God, the purpose of our passage here on earth, and life after death. Josué, who in a kind of trance, watched him constantly from a dark corner of the room, felt as though this sickness was inhaling human beings the way one star might swallow up another. The whole family began going to church every day. They begged the Lord to spare Brad, the family's pride, in exchange for all sorts of exemplary behaviour. They lost their voices on Sundays, singing themselves hoarse while belting out the gospels. In the room where the invalid lay, Davina had set up a small altar decorated with pictures of Christ and Brad, with incense and musical scores. During this time, everyone noted that rain was pouring into the neighbourhood at will, no longer kept at bay by Brad's exhilarating music.

After several futile attempts, Josué finally managed to have a doctor visit the house. He, a man in his seventies who came walking along the park, his bag in hand, sporting a goatee and a monocle, confirmed what Davina had said: as the illness had severely damaged his respiratory system, Brad was dying. He was breathing so strenuously that he seemed to want to fill his lungs with all the air in the world. When the doctor told the family that this sickness was called the white plague, Josué didn't contradict him, afraid that he would leave, but in his heart of hearts he knew that the disease had everything to do with cannibal stars and very little to do with the plague.

One night, with the moon as full as a light bulb, Brad, stretched out on his bed, his hands joined upon his breast, breathed his last. Josué opened his mouth to give voice to his pain, but his mute cry never passed his lips. He rushed to the bathroom; looking at his double in the mirror, he saw that not only had he lost his use of words, but that his face would from now on remain expressionless. He wept in silence, to all appearances uncaring. Why, he wondered every day for the rest of his life, did the Lord choose to take away the child of whom he was the most proud? Was it for that very reason, because he so openly preferred Brad to the others? It seemed to him then that God, like an underhanded boxer, took pleasure in delivering blows below the belt. Never again would he utter another word, and it was not his employers who were going to complain, because as one of them remarked in Josué's very presence the following Monday, one perfectly muzzled employee was better than two who spoke.

Leaning over her dead son, Davina wiped the tears from her cheeks and went to her kitchen, where she began pacing up and down, mumbling words that only she could understand. She gesticulated in a way no one had ever seen, at times overcome by emotion, smiling as if she were recalling happy memories and even bursting into laughter as though someone had just told her a good joke. At dawn, after having confirmed Brad's death, the doctor with the goatee, as a precaution, examined all the other members of the family. His face beset by nervous tics, he twitched his nose from bottom to top as he tapped Oscar's chest and belly. After endless auscultations, he told his parents that he wanted to submit him to a battery of tests, and asked them to come to the hospital at the end of the day so that they might get a report on the state of his health.

Davina spent the day murmuring that even if God's will was sometimes obscure, the suffering it generated elevated the soul of mortal man. It's said that she made her way to church to seal a secret pact with Him. Back home, as soon as she stepped into the living room, she told the family members that, not being born yesterday, she knew perfectly well what to expect: Oscar would not be leaving the hospital for some time. Josué raised himself up in his chair and opened his mouth, not, however, to produce a sound. His wife's cheeks were carved out with deep furrows. As he questioned her with his eyes, she replied that she'd had no choice, that if she'd not agreed to sacrifice ten years of her life, Oscar's would not have been saved, it was as simple as that. Josué approached her to explore the accelerated inroads time had made. His eyes filled with tears that bathed his utterly stoic face, and it seems certain that from that moment on his love for his wife grew tenfold.

At day's end, as twilight set fire to the sky, Oscar stood next to the doctor with the goatee, facing Davina and Josué in an office cluttered with plastic thoraxes of all different sizes. He said goodbye to his parents with a wave of his hand, since he was forbidden to embrace them—a moment of implacable cruelty that he would recall many years later. Was it then that there opened up, like a poinciana flower in spring, the wound that would lend him a more inward-looking temperament, essential to artistic creation? Josué contemplated him with his customary blank expression, while Davina, without interrupting the passionate exchange she pursued with her indwelling voices, waggled her fingers next to her ear like an eight-year-old girl before turning her back. His parents dwindled away behind the glass between the office and the corridor; drops of rain dotted the little window giving onto the hospital courtyard; Oscar thought of Brad and the way he could alter the weather with his music, and all at once he found himself wondering if up to then he'd not been taking his life too lightly.

2

Oscar was bound night and day to his hospital bed, as still as a coconut palm under a blazing sun, since he was forbidden any physical activity. It's said that, bored to death, he lived in a world of disjointed dreams, imagined memories, and invented stories with himself as the hero. Over and over he saw himself racing through the neighbourhood streets once again, a kite string in his hand, while far off, beyond the factories' foul exhalations and the rows of teetering houses, a train whistle signalled an end to his freedom. He wondered if he'd ever really walked those teeming avenues where the smell of jerk chicken was able to smother that of soot. He saw himself ambling along the one street that never slept, whose heart pulsed to the strum of a double bass and the blinking of neon signs, or creeping up to a jazz bar's window to clear it of condensation and hearing in the background, like something out of a premonitory dream, Brad's inimitable boogie-woogie, but he never saw Brad because either an ardent music lover leapt to his feet to applaud or a cigarette girl passed through, screening him from sight. When he opened his eyes, aghast at being back on reality's solid ground, he saw his neighbours, dozens of children as sick as himself, all similarly plagued by this illness which, as his father had said, drew you down into a dark void. When one child coughed, he too was wracked by a furious coughing fit, certain each time that it would never stop. Draped in their black veils, the nuns, like crows, circled the room, and was it his imagination playing games, or did they only approach him after having dealt with all the other boys? Was he going mad, or did they all stare past him as if he were a ghost? Had he been swallowed up by his sickness's black hole, *bloodseed*? When, years later, the details of his hospital stay became a subject of conversation, old Jackson couldn't help having her say with her usual tact: Those lovers of little Jesus who don't nurse a child for the reasons we know, I'd have given them a good kick in the rear!

After a few months, once he was feeling better, those same nuns began, in the late afternoon, to roll his bed to a games room where he was allowed to sit in a rocking chair, to push a wooden airplane, and to play checkers with a child who was in just as bad shape as he was. He kept nodding off, and then, with a thread of cool saliva snaking down his cheek, woke to a silence barely disturbed by the constant breath of an overhead fan, in a games room swathed in shadow. He pulled the curtain aside to gaze through the window at the soft moonlight, mirror of time, and the moths trying vainly to shorten their lives by throwing themselves at the streetlight near the entrance. It was then, thinking about the frightening number of his neighbours who vanished every week, that he saw, behind his eyes, advancing towards him, the sniggering skeleton with its enormous scythe, and he wondered, transfixed, what might await him in the realm of the dead. It appears that, rather than conjuring angels reclining at ease on helium-inflated clouds, he dreamt each night that he was clearing a path with a machete through a stifling jungle that swarmed with wild animals snarling and poised to attack and insects that left glistening trails in their wake. Was the All Powerful dooming him to conjure these hostile places because his faith was not sufficiently strong?

They say that one night he got out of bed, tottering, in the games room. Yawning, he turned on the light and stood in the middle of the room without knowing quite what to do, until his eyes came to rest on the drawers of a large wardrobe. He knelt down in front of the piece of furniture to rummage around inside and came across an object that was familiar to him but that at first he couldn't identify. It was a rectangular box of worn mahogany with a latch that he lost no time in opening. What appeared was an organ that reminded him of the one his father had played in times past when he was a sailor, the same one on which Brad had learned his scales. Why did the instrument's keys strike him so differently? Why did they glow with such a seductive brightness? As he later recounted, he would spend the rest of his life asking himself these questions, pondering the troubling irony of having dedicated his entire life to music while remaining utterly oblivious to the deepest roots of his vocation. He tinkled a bit to acquaint himself with the instrument's sound and played an exercise he found on its music stand, then a second, then began a piece for children. A nurse burst into the room, expertly slid the organ back into the wardrobe, and, without saying a word, rolled Oscar's bed to his room. The next day he played the organ again, but for longer, and two days later he played for hours without anyone interrupting him. All of those who were present had the same impression: he seemed to apply himself to the organ not so much for the pleasure it provided, but because it enabled him to lose track of time, that joker who dragged his feet and filled his veins with the poison, boredom. When he performed in front of the other patients, neither the children's nodding heads nor the crows' black wings marking time on their thighs escaped him.

The doctors let him spend more time at the organ, as long as it didn't slow his recuperation. No matter where you were, in the twilit coolness of the corridors, in the empty entry hall with its damp flagstones, in the cafeteria where the crows greedily downed their thin greenish soup, or in the little chapel where doctors, bags under their eyes down to their cheeks, came to perform their perfunctory genuflections, you heard his boogie-woogie airs echoing through the hospital like the promise of a distant future. People sat around him, a spark of hope lodged in their pupils. Was it true, then? Did music have occult powers, as his mother claimed? If not, how to explain that, invisible, he had suddenly become visible? He noted this change as much in the eyes of the staff as in those of his neighbours, even as they were lost in the haze of their own convalescence. These first reactions to his music, although he was still taking baby steps, imprinted themselves forever, it would appear, in his memory. Music did much more than soothe the soul, it enabled mortals, for the time of a performance, to cherish their life in all its twilit decline.

One night in the games room, while rain pounded down and Oscar was playing a ragtime tune he'd learned by ear, a nebulous shadow appeared at his side. Oscar kept on as if nothing had happened, and only turned his head towards the silhouette once he'd finished. It was a girl his age with coal-black hair and a face so milky-white that it seemed vampiric. She had to have been new, he'd never seen her before. When she said to him, in an astonishingly mature voice, You, you play to lose yourself, he didn't know how to reply. Her eyes, shadowed as they were, still had something merry about them, as if her bursts of enthusiasm were tempered by a precocious fatalism. She'd spent a good part of the afternoon listening to him; his music had become her oxygen, and the better it became, the more it filled her lungs.

They began to meet every evening in the games room to share pieces of music that were to their taste. As if her bouts of sickness prevented her from playing to full capacity, she did timid interpretations of some of her favourite pieces, all classical airs. Oscar taught her blues scales and the few jazz turns he knew, while she taught him good posture, the right fingering, and arpeggios, those last reminding him, always, of a wave just on the point of breaking. Every Saturday night, in the games room, he would perform before an audience made up of young patients and the staff, who willingly pardoned him his hesitations and false notes.

Sometimes, as if to put to the test Marguerite's pessimism, Oscar played tricks on her: he glued a pen onto a bench that served as her bedside table so that she damaged her fingernails trying to pick it up, or he cranked up her bed so that when she came back from the cafeteria she wasn't able to hoist herself onto the mattress. You're such a child, she said, not so much as a reproach, but as if she regarded his aggressions as signalling a kind of innocence. That night, as he stared at the cracks in the ceiling of his room and his neighbours' coughing fits died away, Oscar wondered what it was, exactly, that he felt for Marguerite.

One evening, as he was waiting for her in the games room, he learned from a crow that Marguerite had changed wards. When he asked her the reason for the move, she warned him not to raise his voice. One day followed another, he lost his appetite, no longer bathed, and even stopped wanting to play the organ. Another night he was dozing in his room, his face turned towards the frenzied cloud of insects swarming the streetlight, when he heard piano music whose source he first thought was a dream wherein majestic beasts, hunched in the shadows, halted their hunt to lend their ears to a muted melody. Then he realized that the sound was wafting through the half-open window like a breeze, and he recognized the delicate touch of Marguerite. He went to the window and saw another window on the top floor of an adjacent pavilion, giving onto a lighted room where, once the piece ended, there appeared Marguerite's silhouette. So began a musical dialogue at a distance, where they expressed their troubled feelings through their choice of music and the way they performed it.

It's said that, during a sleepless night, he overheard the murmurings of two crows who had entered his room to snuff out the oil lamps. If he understood correctly, it was Marguerite's parents who, having learned what company she was keeping, demanded that she be moved to another pavilion. It seems that his first reaction was to ask himself why, after which he became pensive, not moving a hair, feigning a composure he was far from feeling. What was in his thoughts? The unpitying cruelty of the world? Was he paralyzed with sadness, as his detractors claim? That's doubtless an exaggeration, given O.P.'s combative personality, which he was just beginning to affirm. Was he, on the contrary, channelling his mounting anger into creative energy, as his admirers would insist? This idea, seductive as it is, leaves one perplexed: you don't play an instrument because you're aggrieved, rather you attack the keys because touching them gives you pleasure, that is the true incentive. What is certain is that he was already of an age to sense that the question of race was at the heart of the matter, and what must have come back to him now was surely his father's dimmed eyes on those Friday evenings when he made his way home.

The day he left the hospital, neither his mother, always deep in conversation with her inner voices, nor Oscar, still in a state of shock in the wake of this episode, were brimming with joy, and they greeted each other as if they had just been together the day before. As they walked side by side through the summer air, choked by dust because they were repairing the road, his mother urged him to hurry: a few days a week she cleaned rich people's houses, and she had to get back to her employer. As if it were the most normal thing in the world, she picked up where she'd left off just a few moments before, pursuing a passionate exchange with a neighbour only she could see, concerning something dreadful that had happened when she was still living on her native island.

That night, Josué and Davina organized a little party at their home. They invited members of the extended family and some friends. According to Oscar's brothers and sisters, they crowded around to embrace him; the men threw their arms over his shoulders, the women cried out that he was a miracle boy and squeezed his hands. Despite her modest means, Davina had prepared a jerk chicken and a plate of rice and beans that drew accolades from the guests, as well as some fried plantains that she'd picked up at the West Indian grocer's. Oscar was quizzed about his stay at the hospital, sometimes solemnly, sometimes teasingly, as if people wanted to read between the lines to find out if the personnel had treated him like a poor relative. After the meal, Oscar sat down at the piano and played his heart out while those present looked at each other, amazed. He performed a popular piece with an ease that surprised them all; the keyboard must have seemed enormous compared to the hospital's little organ. After the applause, Prudence, his older sister, remarked that his interest in the piano was fortuitous, since the doctor had forbidden him from playing the trumpet for the time being. Josué went up to him and ruffled his hair before scribbling a phrase in the notebook that now never left his side: *Same pirate, same beard.*

People took the opportunity to question him further, but with tact, so as not to offend him. What exactly had happened at the hospital? He shrugged his shoulders, and kept smiling. Come on, O.P., don't be so coy! He looked about him while twisting his fingers, and as they all sat on the edges of their chairs, he explained that he'd been very bored at the hospital, but thanks to the experiences he'd had, he'd matured by at least ten years. In a joyous cacophony, they showered him with questions: What had he done with his days? Had he made friends with other children? Were there other children from the islands? And the nurses? The doctors? After a while, Oscar got up from his chair and asked Davina if he could excuse himself, he felt faint and wanted to lie down. Once her brother was gone, Prudence, wide-eyed, looked about her and whispered: Am I wrong, or have they sent us back an improved O.P.?

So as not to slip into a bog of indolence, Oscar had taken to reading the hospital's newspapers every day, and he knew that prohibition in the United States had come to an end. Apparently, men of the cloth had been observed taking a drop. After years of imposed sobriety and parched throats, people had protested vehemently in front of the politicians' offices, and they'd at last given in to the angry electorate so that alcohol could once again run free. While he expected to find fewer bars in the neighbourhood, he was astonished to discover that they had multiplied like cats in a cemetery. Cars as long as ocean liners, gleaming like porcelain dishware, glided slowly along the sidewalk; couples dressed to kill strolled arm in arm, stylish and blithe; the mood was electric, imparting the message that those who weren't there were missing out on life.

A few days later, along with his friends, who were treating him with the respect usually reserved for the war-wounded, Oscar gave in to the wishes of one of them and bribed a cook into gaining them entry to the Twilight Station Bar's kitchen. In single file they skirted the employee preparing salads, then the one grilling steaks, and barely dodged the eagle eye of the owner's wife, a stout woman garbed always in a dress bearing the colours of her home island's flag; they took the corridor leading to the artists' dressing rooms, and, as deceptively casual as a lizard who'd just swallowed a cloud of flies, edged into the smoke-filled room where the show was taking place and where a drum solo was reaching its climax thanks to the shuddering cymbals that seemed an artefact of far-off galaxies. Oscar and his friends positioned themselves so they could see the pianist's hands, but a doorman spotted them and shooed them into the street. Once back home, he set himself to reproducing the pianist's phrases until Prudence grabbed him by the ear and dragged him to his room.

Meanwhile, as he complained to all and sundry in a petulant voice, the tedium induced by his school could only be compared to that he had known at the hospital.

However much he laboured over his notebook, he could muster no enthusiasm for the soporific multiplication tables or the irregular verbs with their unpredictable variants. His father slipped into his coat pockets bits of paper with proverbs meant to alter his attitude: grains of rice make for sacks of rice. Oscar nodded yes, but deep within him he saw his father the porter again and again coming home, his uniform bloodied, after having been beaten by a passenger who was "racist"—that was the word he scribbled angrily when his wife asked him what had happened. *Rawtid*, there was no way he was going to become a porter.

Oscar played the piano every morning before leaving for school, at noon in the school's music room, and at home at the end of the day. His father, it's said, was delighted not to have to hound him and administer slaps so he would do his exercises. Was it Oscar's imagination playing tricks on him, or was his mother more sound of mind the longer he sat at the piano, miraculously freed, one might have said, from her stuttering on like a scratched record. One Saturday morning, if one could believe Prudence, while he was practising his C-major arpeggios and had pulled on a brown shirt and grey pair of pants having belonged to Brad, Davina came into the room, stopped short, and went as white as the inside of a coconut. It's not possible, she managed to say in a little girl's voice. She went over to stroke his face with her trembling hands as if he were Christ himself, and murmured "Brad," until Oscar extricated himself from her embrace. He returned her gaze with a stare that in no way concealed his growing irritation: I'm Oscar, *Mudda*. Oscar.

His measured retort froze Davina where she stood, and though, returning to her kitchen, she did not deviate from her practise of never excusing herself, she never again called him anything else but "Oscar." She wasn't stupid, she confided to her friends, she knew very well that her son's inspiring music set her head in order and silenced the voices bickering there; it was just that from her point of view she didn't have to explain herself to her brood. Shortly after this incident she began again to predict the future, not without causing some consternation among her family members. According to her, Oscar's destiny would lead him to Himalayan heights, but be careful, his journey would be marked by terrible temptations. When Oscar asked her to describe those temptations, she closed her eyes, moaned as if imaginary hands were kneading her shoulders, then said, It's too unclear, I have no answer.

Over the following days, a few people in the neighbourhood were witness to the experiment Oscar was conducting. He sat down and played the piano looking perfectly relaxed, often humming the melody, and having first opened the door to the house, he suddenly rushed outside to see what the weather was like. But from the steps going down to the sidewalk he saw, to his chagrin, that it was neither more nor less sunny than before. *Bloodseed*, what was he doing wrong? Wasn't he now playing just as well as Brad? Was he kidding himself about his talent? He sighed deeply and vowed to work harder. As if to catch Mother Nature unawares, he sometimes pretended to go back inside, then spun around, scanning the skies for something abnormal, but no, there was nothing to report.

The Depression, provoked by Davina's handbag at the bank, had only just ended when another misfortune, also a serious setback, befell the city's population. War broke out in the mother countries, which, frankly, very few people they knew had ever seen, but to which they remained deeply attached, although for reasons that everyone had forgotten. Davina assured the members of her family that this conflict had not escaped her notice; for several weeks she'd been having frequent dreams of dozens of owls hooting their heads off in a concert as mesmerizing as it was diabolical. Only, she hadn't wanted to alarm them. When Chester, one of Oscar's older brothers, declared that he wanted to enrol in the army, his news was greeted with delirious enthusiasm. Oscar, not wanting to be left behind, announced in a trembling voice that he would go with his brother to the military barracks and enlist as well, which provoked another round of cheering. That night, however, he fretted in silence, wondering what had got into him.

The next day, although he had not yet reached the age of majority, he was appalled to learn that even snot-nosed kids like himself could be invited into the ranks. It's said that, at the end of his medical exam, he breathed a sigh of relief when the doctor informed him that his lungs were too weak for him to go off and fight in the trenches. May the white plague be praised, *bloodseed*! he exclaimed inwardly as he left the barracks. Chester, on the other hand, who was healthy as a horse, would be setting off to defend his country, and his parents made him promise to write every day. For the first few months, he kept his word. When they received one of his letters, they all ran to the living room and listened in rapt silence to Prudence reading it aloud, standing in the middle of the room. No one was surprised by his exploits, and even less by his bravery, thanks to which he was able to shoot down dozens of the enemy, win several hand-to-hand battles, and thwart an attack by intercepting enemy radio transmissions. His daring in battle and his resourcefulness were a surprise to no one; after all, he was a worthy member of their family, *rawtid*!

During this time, Oscar's marks at school declined with the regularity of a thermometer at the start of winter. On one of his days off, according to his sisters, Josué tailed his son, either hiding behind a streetcar or in the narrow entrance to a snack bar, when he saw him turning his way. When Oscar took an alleyway, then another, to slip into a neighbourhood bar, Josué had to admit, with some bitterness, that his suspicions were well founded. From what he could tell from the sidewalk, his son was being allowed to practise the piano during the day, when the instrument was free. Right at noon, Oscar made his way to school to have lunch with his friends as if everything was normal, after which he installed himself at the piano in the auditorium for a show that charmed both teachers and students. Apparently, as Josué learned from listening in on a conversation between two of the schoolgirls, that was a daily routine. The realization that his son's entire life centred around the piano hit him like a thunderbolt. After hearing a few pieces, he had to acknowledge, not without a certain pride, that his son, already a celebrity at school, was regarded as a kind of public entertainer you could ask to play any song that was then in fashion. On his way home he began to question his misgivings where his son's passion for the piano was concerned, and that night he told no one about his expedition.

When Chester announced in the postscript to a laconic letter that he might soon be coming home, the family members looked at each other with astonishment, because, if you could trust the news bulletins on the radio, the fight was still raging in the mother countries. One Sunday morning, as the family was getting ready to leave for church, there was a knock at the door, and when they saw him standing there on the rubber doormat, their blood went cold: *rawtid*, he'd lost a hand to that barbarous war! For weeks, the family's morale was lower than low, even though no one talked about it, whether Chester was present or not. But what is this I hear! cried the minister right in the middle of his sermon, having heard about the blow to their family. What is this I hear! he repeated in a ringing voice that made the church windows shake. We must thank the Lord for having spared him on the field of honour! And he launched into a paean—in which he rather lost his way, as often happened—celebrating physical courage and the will to power, which alone could vanquish tyranny and evil! What would Jesus Christ have done in his place, huh? Would he have talked things over with the enemy? He gave a little laugh before going on: You don't talk with the devil, no! This speech gave some comfort to the family members, if only because many of the faithful applauded them in front of the church. But Chester, since his return as sad as raindrops on a grave, took in the familiar faces around him with eyes whose light had been snuffed out.

When Oscar went to a bar in secret to see a pianist playing bebop, the new style of jazz that didn't really appeal to him, there he found Chester. Unrecognizable, in a stupor, he was always with his wolf pack of brothers in arms. Often, making his way between tables, he'd take a punch at someone who'd looked at him askance and rush from the premises to howl into the night that he'd been treated like dirt in the army because he was a "negro." Sometimes he pulled off his clothes to walk stark naked in full view of a pack of revellers doubled up in laughter, before hurling at everyone in sight a volley of curses that made your hair stand up on end. He slept for whole afternoons, often until Oscar came home from school, and barely dressed, wandered into the living room scratching his head and his sex, scandalizing his parents. He asked Oscar to play a frantic boogie-woogie and, after popping open a beer, installed himself in Josué's armchair, fully aware that he was committing a crime of *lèse-majesté*. Bit by bit, he sank into a deep depression, and in the end began to cry while stroking his stump. Oscar stopped playing to approach his brother, but Chester just got angry and ordered him to get lost.

It's said that, after a few weeks of this behaviour, Josué took his notebook and wrote to Chester, in his usual laconic style, "A shepherd divideth his sheep from the goats," before showing him the door. Chester advanced on his father, as if to prove that he could strike him down if he wanted to, and each held the other's gaze without flinching until Chester at last backed off and left the house. That night, her anger barely contained, Davina upbraided her husband in no uncertain terms for having turned away her son. In the name of God, had he forgotten their island ways? Josué, true to himself, remained unmoved. That night, Oscar dreamed that in a deserted alleyway the neighbourhood thugs were beating Chester up, after which, against all expectations, his head bloodied, his eyes protruding from their orbits, he rose up, to the stupefaction of his assailants, who all took to their heels, clacking their teeth like bone-cold skeletons.

Months went by before Chester reappeared, clean-shaven, a wry smile on his lips. He sat himself down on the living room couch and crossed his legs like a gentleman, announcing, with a certain detached pride, that having hit bottom—he was born under a lucky star, you had to believe—Providence had sent his way a Good Samaritan who'd convinced him that he had to make the best of things. Despite his infirmity, the Samaritan had found him an opening in a metallurgical business where he was the union leader. By day, like everyone else, Chester honourably earned his daily bread; at night, he forced himself to curb his taste for alcohol, even if that meant crossing the street when he passed a bar. He'd rented a room a few streets from the family home, determined to make himself a burden no longer. Josué went up to him, expressionless, and for a long while no one knew if he was going to slap him or shake his hand. Finally, he embraced him, and scrawled in his notebook that the door of his house would always be open to him, assuming he'd conquered his demons.

Chester's progress gave Josué so much to think about that one evening he called Oscar and Davina into the living room. As his father scribbled in his notebook, Oscar realized, astounded, that he'd been following him everywhere for months. Did he want to do penance on earth and end up like Chester? Didn't he know that he was heading straight towards poverty and that this was not a desert crossing from which he might emerge victorious? Oscar saw that the time had come to show his mettle. I want to be a pianist, he heard himself say. While he ran through his mind the arguments he would present in the case of a refusal—as a part of the community, the options available to him were limited, and since he didn't want to be a porter or a metalworker, there was only one choice left, the only activity that gave him pleasure—Davina declared that it was normal that he play the piano for a living; would he not be fulfilling Brad's foreshortened destiny? Whether one liked it or not, events would unfold according to an implacable logic, and she reminded the family members, as if it were necessary, that you cannot escape God's will. So it would be foolish not to seize this second chance that was being offered. Josué looked Oscar straight in the eye and scribbled one last sentence: Fine, but promise me that you'll be the one to shine brightest in the firmament of piano jazz. A flash of joy lit up Oscar's face, and he promised to do his best not to dishonour the family.

In the months that followed, Oscar observed that bebop, the new jazz characterized by rapid shifts in tonality, virtuosity, and eccentricity—all manifested in the studied dishevelment of the musicians' clothes—only appealed to a clique. That was not where he was at ease. For him jazz was music both for listening and dancing, an art that brought people together, as in the time of his childhood. One night, when he and Prudence were listening to a special program on CBC Radio featuring the new wave of swing that was taking the country by storm, the host announced a cross-country piano competition. When she suggested he enter, Oscar could see that the contest represented a perfect opportunity, but the prospect of having to perform before thousands of listeners was unnerving, to say the least. Yet when his sister summoned the rest of the family, he swallowed hard and, seeing them all come running, had no choice but to lend himself to the adventure. Did he screw up his courage, hoping against hope that Marguerite would be listening to the broadcast? In any event, he chose to play a ragtime with a heavily syncopated right hand, because he remembered the carefree time when Brad was still the neighbourhood's shooting star, and he, his will-o-the-wisp.

The day of, in a softly lit studio with state-of-the-art microphones, two men in jackets, with artificial smiles, interviewed him before his performance. He knew, did he not, that it wasn't fair for the other contestants, because he had music in his blood? Sardonic sniggering followed. What would he do if he won the prize? Would he help out his family? How did he spend his free time? Could he not see that his community's customs and way of life were largely foreign to his listeners? When he ventured an answer, they interrupted to ask if he had given any thought to what he was saying. Clearly the interview unsettled him. When, seated at the grand piano, he was about to attack the piece he'd tirelessly rehearsed for two weeks, his stomach was in such knots that he became an automaton unable to shade his performance, accelerating pointlessly in the *moderato* passages, playing the *prestissimos* robotically. When he left the studio he ran to the washroom where, snot-nosed, he emptied his guts, and was seized with a vertigo that had the walls reeling around him. His face deathly pale, he waited for hours in the corridor where smartly dressed people came and went. When it was announced that he'd won the competition, he thought it was a bad joke, and showed no enthusiasm when the organizers took turns shaking his hand and presented him with a generous cheque. The studio telephone was ringing off the hook. People adored his style, which made them want to dance and forget their cares; you would have thought we were back in the great days of swing, declared a lady who was bubbling over with enthusiasm. Back home he was greeted with cries of joy and endless accolades. It's said that he choked back as best as he could his sour saliva, visibly saddened that Marguerite had not shown herself as he'd secretly hoped.

The end of the war was marked by a deluge of parties and balls, at which Oscar and his friends desperately wanted to be present, since the great names of swing would be passing through town. But how to set foot in these vast halls without knowing anyone, and being minors and penniless to boot? One night, near a popular cabaret in the centre of town, one of the radio hosts, who had earlier treated him with supreme condescension, saw right away what they wanted; he whispered something in the doorman's ear, who, with a strained smile, invited them in. The scene took their breath away: Benny G., the clarinetist of the hour, was playing, even more unreal and charming than on the radio, and the atmosphere was electric; the music lovers were following the beat, nodding their heads, while the dancers, all spiffed up, moved with a feline grace; finally, the girls, like models out of the magazines, were pretty enough to die for. Oscar followed the pianist's every note and deep inside saw that he could easily take his place, so humdrum was his playing. Johnny H.'s orchestra, the town's most prestigious, then took over the stage, so energized and driven that the musicians played on until dawn. As he later remembered it, Oscar that night determined that his jazz would be swing or nothing.

Soon, against all expectations, the CBC began cozying up to him. The hosts constantly praised his rapid playing, asked him about strides and cadenzas, about his favourite pieces and his hobbies. His neighbourhood was the source for all sorts of questions, as the hosts struggled to believe that O.P. had emerged from this territory where they had never set foot. His answers gave rise to many other queries, and finally it was agreed that he had to be asked back. He was given a late-night show where he first played pieces of his own choice; in the second hour, he invited local musicians into the studio and, despite his youth, schooled the listeners in the rudiments of jazz. When he turned up at a jazz bar with one of his two recently acquired jackets, the owner draped his arm around his shoulders, teased him by letting him know that he was the only minor in town who was accorded such special treatment, and gave him a few taps on the cheek. Musicians who had never deigned to address a word to him rose in his path to introduce themselves, bowing and scraping. Once Oscar left, the envious, secretly pained, lashed out at his success: Why him? He's a lousy interview, no? And a lower blow: If you want my opinion, he's the perfect token Negro.

Impossible not to see it, things were booming since the end of the war. Posters all over the town touted a tsunami of shows: radio stars' names were everywhere on people's lips. You would have thought that this was the advent of a new society, determined that no one would huddle glumly in his corner. You did whatever it took to get each and all strutting their stuff twenty-four hours a day. To hell with the preachers' temperance, our life on earth was just too short. When Oscar shared with Chester his sense of wonder at all these upheavals, his brother just laughed and shot back: No kidding, O.P., the war changed everything. Open your eyes for Pete's sake, it's made the con men rich. And he launched into an analysis of what he called our "society of pimps," where the second-rate and the peddlers of all sorts were praised to the skies, and where it was seen in a positive light to spit on the humblest among us. In short, this society worked on the same principles that governed the relationship between procurers and prostitutes: either you did what you were told and spread your legs to sell what was most precious to you, or you were looked down on because you were poor. It's as simple as that, *bredda*. Oscar listened carefully and felt guilty for not sharing his brother's seething anger towards "the system." Of course, Chester went on, you're in good with them, because your talent helps them to fill their pockets. But watch out, O.P., as soon as they don't need you anymore, they'll drop you like an old shoe.

One night at the CBC studio, while he was slipping his score into his shoulder bag, he received, it's said, a telephone call. Even before the caller introduced himself, Oscar recognized the fast-talking nasal voice of Johnny H., the famous bandleader, who, well known for his straight talk, asked him outright if he wanted to join his group as their regular pianist. Oscar was speechless for long seconds before managing to say that it would give him great pleasure. From that day on, as he had to get up earlier, he sometimes had breakfast with his father, learned two or three pieces on the piano, left for school, marked up his scores during his classes, delighted the crowd at noon, got to the radio studios, was witty during his show, and then made his way to the Ritz-Carlton Hotel, where Johnny H.'s band was rehearsing.

One Saturday morning, during a dress rehearsal, the maître d'hôtel turned up and took Johnny aside. The conversation began quietly, but as soon as Johnny raised his voice, the maître d' began openly to make allusions to Oscar. Several times he said that he couldn't do anything, that he had no choice, that distinguished guests would refuse to attend the show if Oscar were present. Johnny began to laugh, and asked why those people were making such silly demands. Faced with the maître d'hôtel's silence, he turned, and himself singled Oscar out: But look at him, just look at him, he wouldn't hurt a fly. After a moment, the maître d' asked him calmly why he was trying to make things hard for him, he knew very well the reason for the request. Stop playing the innocent, he sighed, and went on like an impatient professor: It's too bad, because up to now it's been a pleasure working with you, but if you stop cooperating, you'll have lost the one thing I require in a band leader. He knew what was hiding behind this ridiculous request, Johnny replied, but he'd wanted him to say it without beating around the bush. The band would only play with Oscar, otherwise they'd all pack up and go. Many years later Oscar told this story, and made it clear that ever since that day, he'd owed a lifelong debt to Johnny. The maître d'hôtel's bright little eyes tensed to send forth daggers, after which he swivelled around and headed down a long corridor overhung by a string of crystal chandeliers.

So what do we do now? asked one of the trombones. We keep rehearsing, what else? Johnny shot back. One hand over his half-open mouth, Oscar for a long time didn't move a muscle or reply to the questions he was asked. According to what he himself said, it was only then that he realized that he was the only black member of the band. Had he lost the last vestige of his innocence? Or on the contrary, did he resolve that a certain innocence, salutary and essential, would always be vital to the music he made? Those long familiar with Oscar's music may provide the answer.

That same evening, an hour before the performance, the hotel owner himself phoned Johnny to tell him it was all a misunderstanding that should be immediately forgotten. That night, while the guests were stuffing themselves with snow crab swilled down with champagne, Oscar played with such furious virtuosity that he had the crowd on their feet for each of his solos. Once the show was over, as Johnny was treating the band members to a meal offered by the hotel, Oscar got his belongings together, pulled on his raincoat, and disappeared. Johnny rushed into the street to catch him. On the sidewalk, in the middle of a night lit by brand new electric streetlamps, and while dozens of cars trailed each other bumper to bumper along the road, the bandleader told him not to let himself be humiliated by an imbecile, that it wasn't worth the trouble. O.P. replied that he appreciated the way he'd managed the situation, but really, he preferred to be alone. Okay, but don't forget that the band needs you, Johnny called after him as Oscar moved away.

At the street corner, he raised the collar of his raincoat, walked at a brisk pace, and according to those close to him, as the first drops began to fall, he thought of Brad. He'd perhaps never be able to match the mathematical beauty of his playing, but, it would appear, the very act of thinking about his dead brother brought peace to his heart. A few steps later, he was asking himself if his imagination was playing tricks on him, or if the models of the cars driving by were really ten years out of date. A bit farther still, was he mistaken, or were the women he passed really wearing the kind of coats you used to see years ago? And then, why, in the shop windows, did he not see any of the vacuum cleaners and fans that only yesterday he'd noticed everywhere? Had his music disrupted both time and his own perceptions?

When he got onto the streetcar, it seemed that the effect of the music had already weakened; only half the passengers were wearing clothes from the age of swing. He then experienced an awakening both rude and cheering; though his heart was bleeding, his breast swelled with the sense of a mission accomplished. As he walked towards the back of the car, a few passengers stared at him doubtfully, others with indifference or sympathy. Had it always been that way? When he got down from the tram and strolled along, as much to take the air as to observe the passersby, there was no one, anymore, wearing clothes that brought back his cherished childhood years. As he advanced, head down, he tried in vain to unscramble his ideas, and to free himself from the anguish that tightened his throat. He arrived in his neighbourhood and entered·his house.

The next day he attended church with his whole family. When the minister saw him among the faithful, he strayed from his sermon to vaunt the virtues of persistence. Without pronouncing Oscar's name, he stressed how important it was for members of the community to step up and to serve as examples. We need models, God's chosen, he added. What effect did these words have on Oscar? Was it nigh, the day when they'd no longer be looked down on like the plague, like less than nothing? continued the reverend. He truly wanted to know. Of course, we must arm ourselves with patience, our earthly paradise is not for tomorrow, and he emitted a laugh that stopped short just as fast, as if the flush of hope his reflections inspired had just met reality's hard wall. Once the service was over, there were many who approached Oscar outside the church, girls to give him a kiss, men to shake his hand. As he later said, it was then that it first sank in that from now on he'd be addressed with the same deference as the community's leaders.

3

Now Oscar had the wind behind him, and for those keeping track of his exploits it would have been hard to imagine that he was heading for a moral crisis that would bring him to his knees, transfixed by self-doubt. But that is to get ahead of ourselves. During this period, everyone in the neighbourhood who followed him, sometimes with amazement, sometimes wracked by envy, was wondering if he didn't possess the gift of being everywhere at once. As soon as his radio broadcast was over he hailed a taxi to rush to the Ritz-Carlton, where, invariably, he stole the show from the other members of Johnny H.'s band, then dashed out to grab onto a careening streetcar heading to the lower town, got off at an intersection in the neighbourhood from which the alluring hubbub of the jazz bars could already be heard, and entered the Twilight Station with a small satisfied smile on his lips. It was there that, night after night, to sold-out crowds, he gave of himself heart and soul, confident that the music he was making was unique, in that it married the unifying spirit of swing to the intimate feel of the small group he led, a trio made up of piano, double bass, and drums; that was where, brick by brick, he was laying the foundations for his musical world.

It so happened that when Oscar was in his groove, odd things occurred that would have stunned a client wandering all unawares into the bar: all the women seemed to have agreed among themselves to wear long dresses and hats that would have been in vogue ten years earlier; the men, without exception, had pulled on baggy pants the likes of which you no longer saw, some going so far as to sport tweed caps, just like those of yesteryear. Both men and women, most of them, had rummaged in their attics in search of cigarette holders, holding them limply, as was proper, between the index and middle finger, so that the most pungent of aromas, just like those of the previous decade, permeated the room. Everyone drank gin cocktails like in the old days, and if you looked over your shoulder at a client leaning on the bar, you thought your eyes were playing tricks on you, because he was reading a newspaper ten years out of date. When, late in the night, the tables were pushed against the wall, people danced as they had in the past, with the same steps, the same gesticulations, and the same air of feigned incredulity, fed by a despairing energy that sought in movement, or so it seemed, to erase the trauma occasioned not by the Second World War, but by the First. What beat all, however, were the clients around tables who were exchanging ten-year-old memories as if they were events that had just occurred that very day. People setting foot in the bar for the first time were instantly transfixed; they asked the doorman, seriously, if all the customers were actors engaged in the dress rehearsal for a naturalistic play. At the first sign of dawn the avid music lovers dispersed, heading home, where some in their dreams prolonged their immersion in a long-gone world, before opening their eyes to a wash of the morning's grey light, realizing, to their chagrin, that the magic had ceased to operate, and that Oscar's music had faded away.

The newspapers outdid each other in eloquence and went overboard with their superlatives to incite the public to attend his shows, even though he hadn't yet made a record. According to the critic of a French-language daily, Oscar's jazz, never before seen, was something so perfect that it was the very embodiment of the city's pulse. Another, a grouchy anglophone who had always longed for the great American cities, wrote: Who would have believed it, but at the heart of this lacklustre city, at the centre of its most unsavoury neighbourhood, and I'll be damned if I could have foreseen such a miracle, there has been born out of the most abject mire, if I may term it thus, a genius, a true genius, I tell you! His playing was scrutinized in its every detail; all agreed on his matchless virtuosity, his music's verve, his technical prowess, his fingers' outright gymnastics—but was he an innovative pianist? How did he compare with New York's bebop piano players, like the impetuous Bud P. who played with Charlie P., the shooting star of jazz saxophonists? Which is all to say that the ongoing debates surrounding the merits of his playing, which followed him all through his career, began very early on.

Meanwhile, it seemed that not a day went by without his thinking about Marguerite. Sunday afternoons, when he was free, there were many who saw him wandering alone, hands in the pockets of his raincoat, a fedora shading one eye. He advanced at random, but always ended up heading for the affluent neighbourhoods. There, he spent hours contemplating the castle towers on the mountainside, and in this dreamy state he meandered, once night had fallen, past the rich houses, to gaze on the windows opening into rooms with crystal chandeliers and muted light, imagining living there with Marguerite. He edged up to a house, his eyes wide, as if swearing to the gods above that the young woman seen from behind with her ebony hair really was Marguerite; but when the girl turned to reveal an angular profile, he sadly bowed his head. That could happen several times over in one night, so that by the time he turned for home he was exhausted and as downcast as could be. In the moonlight and under the luminous cone of a streetlamp, as if to shield himself from this sorrow that reached into his very depths, he tried to persuade himself to associate with other women, such as those, for example, who hovered about him after his shows.

As soon as he stepped outside, his childhood friends descended on him: what a pleasure to see him, because, seriously, O.P., were they ever proud of him! Oscar smiled politely, throwing a quick glance at his watch, and hey, you're not going to start dodging us, are you? And him coming out with a forced laugh, pretending to be fascinated by the distant, stormy horizon over the mountain: No, of course not, but a guy's got to earn his keep, no? Of course, O.P., but don't forget us, that's all we're asking. We'll go to your show at the Twilight Station next week, and we'll have a couple of drinks together, like in the good old days, right? And while he was shaking hands with everyone to say goodbye, someone invariably came up to him: Don't want to bother you, but you wouldn't have some money or a cigarette, by any chance? Oscar was uncomfortable, his expression shifting from the sudden anger flushing his cheeks to a brotherly compassion, until finally he groped in his pockets and held out a few coins. O.P., you're the best, and, once he was far enough away, Really, success hasn't gone to his head, not one bit.

Every Sunday he went to church. It was good for him, it gave him the feeling that all his stress was slipping away, as he told his close companions. He saw that environment, crucial to his maintaining his mental balance, as the complement to the womb-like ambiance of the bars. There he worshipped with fervour, singing the gospels full-throated and sometimes going so far as daring, in all solemnity, to weep. He conscientiously recited the psalms, pausing at each word as if to grasp its hidden meaning so that divine mercy, mysterious, would enter into him. What was he seeking? What was going on in his precocious brain? Was he asking himself if he was an elect like Brad, as the reverend in his sermons claimed every time the occasion presented itself? Was God really looking down on him with benevolence? Had He invested him with a noble mission, to be a model for his community? Oscar sighed and bowed his head, it was hard to bear, all that. Oh, of course, like anyone else he would have preferred that God manifest himself unambiguously, if only through some object surreptitiously displaced. Lost in the maelstrom of these questions, he would suddenly notice a girl, usually rather plump, squinting in his direction with a kind of dreamlike longing, and it was only when he talked to her outside the church that he realized that she was a friend from primary school or a neighbour with whom he'd once read the comics in the daily paper.

It's said that one Sunday morning, he felt the warmth on his cheeks of one of those vaporous gazes, and, turning his head, he was deeply troubled at the sight of a girl on the other side of the aisle with curly hair, high cheekbones, and eyelashes like ski slopes. This beauty drew his eyes to her with such intensity that he felt as if he were being flung in her direction. But who was this apparition? Outside the church, one of his friends informed him that her name was Beverly and that her family, more affluent than those of the neighbourhood, had just moved in nearby. He didn't even have to manoeuvre to meet her: she'd arranged for a common friend to introduce them. She was flirtatious, nicely turned out, and, it seemed, adventurous. For their first date, he invited her to a popular diner in the centre of town, where there were wine-red banquettes and a windowed facade from which you could watch the passersby. She was a good girl, who dreamed of one thing only: starting a little family with a faithful man. Knowing she was attractive and from a good family, she had set her cap for Oscar, beyond dispute the local star. Three months later to the day, as the first winter storm whitened the city's rooftops and Beverly was at the Ritz-Carlton attending one of his shows, he knelt before her in front of the public and his colleagues to ask for her hand. When, her voice trembling, her eyes wet, she accepted, there followed a salvo of applause, and the same people who'd once opposed his playing under that roof came up to congratulate him, holding out their hands, a gesture to which Oscar, swallowing his pride, responded graciously, in appearance at least. Four months later, a week after he had attained his majority, they were wed in the neighbourhood church before a minister who seemed about to levitate with joy. It seems that that very night, she lowered her drawbridge, onto which Oscar threw himself with the ardour of an inexperienced young man accustomed to very short-lived pleasures. They bought a pretty white wooden house in the neighbourhood, a few streets away from that of O.P.'s parents. When their first child was born, Oscar, filled with anxiety at the prospect of being responsible for a life other than his own, wondered if he'd not made an irreparable mistake. The years that followed proved him wrong: his children, with whom he occupied himself very little, in no way impeded his artistic success.

To his already very busy schedule, he added courses with a prestigious teacher of classical music, a student of a student of Liszt, a man so thin that he seemed always to be in profile. While Oscar played, the teacher placed glasses of water on the backs of his hands to train him in maintaining good posture, to the point where, his pants as drenched as if he had spilled his soup, O.P. invariably caught cold after his lessons. Meanwhile, he continued to work on his orchestral piano style, raising his virtuosity to levels never before seen, in the opinion of the city's cranky critic. What was his problem with the bebop pianists? he asked him in an interview. Ignoring the left hand, and dabbling in a music that marginalized jazz and that would sooner or later entail its death.

In those years, as 78 rpm gave way to 45, the music industry thrived, placing itself in the foreground of the arts and entertainment world. The public's appetite seemed insatiable, the clubs and cabarets were never empty, and radio, according to some, was experiencing its golden age. How could one foresee that a few years later, the advent of television would put an end to radio's dominance? Many businessmen, seeing a good deal in the offing, threw themselves headfirst into the adventure of opening a local branch for a record company based usually in the United States.

Oscar's reputation was such that he was not surprised to receive a phone call at home from a local producer who wanted to record his music. As he later told the story, the man was a potbellied individual of few words, wracked by nervous tics, who constantly spilled coffee onto his pants and shirt, but who seemed not to think anything of it. O.P. was so delighted at the idea of making a recording that with doglike docility he agreed to all the producer's conditions for fear that this strange man might change his mind. After a few meetings, the fidgety producer held out the record jacket for a disc where you could read "Oscar P." in big letters and, on the other side, the list of pieces that had been picked out for him. Oscar was speechless, and the deal was done.

The disc was a commercial success of sorts, despite the lamentable quality of the recording—it sounded like Oscar was playing at the other end of the room from the microphones—and despite the producer's serious inability to boost sales. One day, when the producer got up to serve himself yet another cup of coffee, Oscar couldn't help reading, upside down, a letter sitting on his desk. A representative of the mother company was expressing his puzzlement at the tic-riddled producer's refusal to cede the recording's rights to Oscar so that it could be distributed in the United States. O.P. left the office, never to return. Inquiring as to the producer's reputation among more experienced musicians, he learned that the man had behaved the same way with others, because he himself hoped to distribute their records worldwide, even if he did almost nothing to realize this ambition. When she told the story to whoever paused in front of her house to chat a little, old Jackson would end it thus: Our O.P. soon got the message that a goat with no cunning won't fatten up.

One bitterly cold night, as he was finishing up his last show at the Twilight Station, he thought he spotted out of the corner of his eye a certain Dizzy G., a crony of Charlie P. and a trumpet player of note, who was listening with a thoughtful air, seated at a table where there were half a dozen musicians. According to what Oscar later said, when the show was over Dizzy got up to congratulate him and invited him for a drink. After two beers, he asked him if he could speak frankly and suggested that he drop his boogie-woogie repertoire, that it was an outdated style that constricted him. Keep to swing, to ballads, that's what shows off your talent, *bredda*. From one glass to the next, without knowing quite how, they found themselves upstairs engaged in a lively conversation with some scantily clad girls, and each of them ended up in a different room with one of the ladies. As the girl was unbuttoning her blouse, stretched out before him like a warm sand beach, Oscar kept thinking about Dizzy's advice; if he'd understood rightly, he'd go nowhere if he didn't sign with an American record company.

Oscar and Dizzy left the bar at the break of day, laughing arm in arm, not so much because of the alcohol, but because of the ice that had turned the sidewalk into a skating rink. Dizzy, who'd lost track of his musician friends, was hoping to sleep for a few hours before catching the train that would bring him back to New York. He readily accepted Oscar's invitation to stay with him. It's said that on the doorstep in her dressing gown, Beverly, who hadn't slept all night, when she saw that he'd been drinking and that he wasn't alone, glared at Oscar through swollen eyes as if to wipe him off the face of the earth. She was busy sniffing his breath when she noticed the lipstick smudge on his shirt collar. It's not what you think, mumbled Oscar, while, with his hand flat against the wall, Dizzy was trying hard not to laugh. Beverly's eyes went moist and filled with tears, triggering a gale of laughter from Dizzy. Oscar then did something that was unlike him, and he did it for that very reason: imitating Dizzy, he too doubled up laughing. Beverly returned to her room, and that morning the men went to sleep at a hotel.

Every time Oscar ran into his old neighbourhood friends, someone asked him for money, and every time, he searched his pockets and held out a coin or a bank note, knowing that he'd never be reimbursed. Why did he keep doling out money? Was he a prisoner of his fine-fellow image? It was perhaps then, for the first time, that he had the seductive idea of leaving the neighbourhood. One morning, a childhood friend of whom he'd lost track, a little man who was having a hard time making ends meet as a saxophonist, in part because he was doing heroin in the Twilight Station toilets, perhaps to emulate his bopper idols—he'd called O.P.'s music old-fashioned—had the nerve to appear on Oscar's doorstep with his wife and children. It's to feed my family, O.P., come on, he implored in a broken voice. Looking down from his bouncer's height, Oscar glared at him as if he wanted to run him through with his gaze's invisible lance, and then slammed the door in his face.

One Saturday afternoon, as the sun was ending its job of transforming the snow banks into runnels, Josué and Oscar went down towards the port, zigzagging through the maze of narrow streets. Earlier that day, if you can believe his sisters, when his father suggested taking a walk, Oscar began to worry: his father, when he wasn't onboard a train, spent most of his time with his nose buried in an astronomy manual or sitting in the living room listening to his favourite records, and in truth, he almost never went walking. A boat was at anchor in the port, full of immigrants waving to the crowd with their handkerchiefs. It had apparently crossed the ocean in five weeks after having braved the fury of a dozen storms. His father leaned on the railing, breathed in the air, and contemplated the awestruck faces of the new arrivals with his customary impassivity. After they'd installed the gangplank, the immigrants filed down, their weighty bags on their backs, two or three suitcases in their hands, inadequately dressed, their children hanging onto the women's long skirts. When the boat was finally emptied, Josué pulled out his notebook to scribble a message that he held out to his son: I'm up to my neck in unpaid bills. He fixed the horizon with his emotionless eyes before writing another note: I'm tearing my hair out. Oscar placed a hand on his father's shoulder: Don't worry, I'll take care of everything. Josué warmly thanked his son, promised to pay the money back as soon as possible, and shared this thought with him: The bird of paradise sets down only on generous hands.

Every other Friday night, Oscar's brothers and sisters, along with their little families, came to eat at their parents'. They all gathered in the cramped kitchen where the steam from Davina's cooking pots clouded the windows, while the children, swift as eels, dodged between them, playing hide-and-seek. The men, sitting around the table, one hand on a thigh, the other holding a cold beer, chewed away at bread that they dipped in an outlandishly spicy sauce; the women talked standing up near the counter and then burst out laughing, frantically waving their hands as if they were suffering from third degree burns. Those who unwisely tried to offer Davina some help found themselves summarily rebuffed, set back on their heels by her no-nonsense dismissals. When there were not enough chairs, the men surrendered their places to the ladies and ate standing up at the counter, which exasperated Davina. Josué, who disapproved of her larger-than-life reactions, got up to write and pass notes to his wife, who, without even reading them, tossed them to the floor while raising her eyes to heaven, after which the brothers and sisters, together, burst out laughing.

That was when Chester, it seems, shifted the conversation to the bosses and the deep contempt they inspired in him, keeping things playful, usually, and addressing his companion, a different woman from one Friday to the next. He described in detail their unbelievable self-importance, their arrogant indifference, their limitless egoism, and their inherent avarice. As no one took seriously his concept of a "society of pimps," he patiently expounded, brooking few interruptions, a schematic class theory which, according to him, harmonized well with the principles of roulette, dooming the most destitute to lose and lose again, while fattening the bourgeois. He paused to catch his breath and take a mouthful of beer, after which he began to rail against those who turned their backs on the unions. The others exchanged uneasy glances and didn't say a word, for fear of incurring his wrath. Gesticulating aggressively, he then addressed himself to Oscar, asking him if the musicians had finally united so as not to be conned by the bosses, and when his brother didn't reply, he reminded him of his disastrous experience with the producer, an episode that was off limits for the family.

Despite the rich establishments he frequented and the generous girth that had him resembling his bosses,

Oscar was just a servant, and he'd better not forget it. The proof was that the salary he received was a thousand times smaller than that of the producers, promoters, and club owners. Indirectly, Oscar was complicit, because his shows helped drive the mad machine that bled the workers. Chester raised himself up briefly, as if to give himself courage, took a good swig of beer, and was off again: yes, because of his inaction and his wilful blindness, he was complicit in the crimes committed in the name of capital. Then one night, according to his sisters, Oscar had had enough, and he reminded Chester that he had always, in his own way and with his certainly modest means, helped out all those who were in need, perfectly aware that life was not rosy for most people. How can you attack me like that? Me, your brother? As Chester went on blaming him for the fate of thousands of individuals, Oscar cut him short: Who did Papa go to when he was in need? Do you know? It's strange, he didn't go to you, the great champion of the workers, but to me, the accomplice in capitalism's crimes. Isn't that bizarre? And then, as everyone—including Davina— wanted to know what exactly he was talking about, Oscar described in detail the afternoon he spent in his father's company at the port, under the neutral gaze of the man in question and while Chester was accusing him of creating a cowardly diversion.

Back home, Beverly put the two children to bed—a second had just been born. She stretched out under the blankets and called Oscar, who had stayed behind in the living room, listening to the radio. It's said that he was beside himself, hurt by the words of Chester, who, to his mind, couldn't tolerate his success. A thought went through his mind that the old proverb took on all its meaning when its terms were reversed: the happiness of one makes for the unhappiness of others. He wanted to take the air, he told his wife, who got up to ask him anxiously where he intended to go at that late hour. As he remained silent, she said, in a more conciliatory tone: What's happening with you, O.P.? She was getting all worked up over nothing, she was dramatizing a situation that had nothing dramatic about it. She went silent in her turn before lashing out, You want to become a druggie, a degenerate like your musician friends, is that it? You're saying whatever comes into your head; you ought to shut up instead of insulting people better than you. Her face froze, she turned away. Do you take me for an idiot, or what? You think I don't know you're going to see that woman who gets her rouge on your shirt? He stared at her for a long time; what was he thinking? Was he asking himself how the refined and dignified woman who had stolen his heart had in such a short time turned into a shrew? Yes, he replied, in a voice that was almost gentle, I'd rather spend the night with a whore than with you. At least there, things are clear, I pay and they give me what I want. He slammed the door behind him; once outside, he pulled up his coat collar. He went to the Twilight Station, less to listen to the music than to spend the night in the arms of the lady of the night in question, to whom he'd given no thought whatsoever before his wife brought her into the conversation. In the morning, when he awoke, he was no doubt surprised that he felt not an ounce of remorse; decidedly, his strength of character impressed him.

One morning, when he was visiting his parents, he had a coffee with his father, who considered him with his affectless eyes before moving into the living room. Oscar followed, and when he saw on the piece of furniture where the radio was enthroned the record cover where he was smiling broadly in a three-quarters portrait, he began strutting, puffing himself up like a peacock. His father scribbled a few words in his notebook: Do you enjoy betraying me, or what? Oscar forced himself to plant a smile on his face: I don't know what you're talking about, *Fadda*. But his father, who wasn't done, ripped several more pages out of his notebook. He reminded him that he had asked him specifically not to say anything about the loan. Did he know that Davina had kept him up all night, questioning him about this business? Did he not yet know that one's word was sacred? Oscar swallowed his saliva.

Thinking that the conversation was almost over, and wanting to avoid its becoming even more acrimonious, Oscar went looking for the raincoat he'd left in the kitchen, but on his return to the living room, Josué had settled into his armchair to listen to a record he'd just placed on the turntable. When a piano riff began, Oscar went quiet, his hands in the pockets of his coat, his brand new fedora on his head, all ears. The melody, like a player piano veering out of control, took off in a dramatic headlong dash, as if the opening were an irritant to the pianist. After a series of strange chords, wilfully dissonant, which brought to mind someone's struggling to maintain his balance, the left hand launched into a blistering, even frenetic rhythm. Oscar, who'd never heard such music, such a sound, such rhythmic complexity at the piano, said to himself—at least that's what his sisters later claimed—that it had to be two pianists, since more than four melodic lines were interacting, coming together, moving in concert for a while only to separate, distance themselves, advance at different tempos. The melodies undeniably constituted a whole, a world both coherent and unsettling. Soon the music mutated into an infectious carnival, but darkly hued, intensely fraught, as if the pianist were playing with a gun to his head. Later, it suggested a shower of meteorites that set everything ablaze, fields of grain, pine forests cast into a deceptive tranquillity, a northern town shuddering under the assaults of a polar freeze.

The piece having ended, Josué let the needle bump up over and over against the label at the centre of the record. Before Oscar had time to ask all the questions boiling up within him, Josué wrote: You're wrong, it's only one pianist. It's said that at that instant, Oscar felt the ground giving way beneath his feet, whereupon Josué stunned him with another revelation: And he's blind. What was Oscar thinking at that moment? It's not easy to know, but we can assume that the damage he inwardly sustained changed his view of the world forever, veiling it with a grey film that from then on would cast a pall over all people and all things. Oscar had enough strength to totter to the phonograph and lean down; the pianist had a strange name, Art T. He dragged himself to the door and left without saying goodbye to his father.

That day, all his listeners learned that Oscar had been replaced as his program's host. The telephone rang off the hook at his home, but not even Beverly knew where he was. A few witnesses claimed to have seen him meandering through the centre of town. Apparently, as he was paying no attention to where he was going, he bumped into several passersby, who, furious, turned to insult him. According to one of the neighbours who crossed his path, you would have said that the commotion inside his head was blinding him to the people around him. Some claimed that he abruptly turned into a record store. Before the morning was out, he'd listened to all the Art T. recordings that he'd been able to find. His face, it was said, fell a bit more with each piece, as if Art's superhuman and unreal performances were snuffing out one by one his artistic ambitions and his claim to be one of the elect. He apparently threw a few bills onto the counter and left the store, leaving the records behind.

No one knew where he spent the night, but over the course of the week a number of people saw him wandering like a lost soul near the train station and sitting on the parks' yellow lawns under this spring's lowering skies. He advanced, dragging his feet. He occasionally raised his eyes to follow, irate, other pedestrians, or, when he crossed paths with a sandwich-man, he wrinkled his nose as if filled with disgust. It's said that, at the end of the day, he went home. But after having criss-crossed the city's streets, he couldn't close his eyes, and he got up to drift from one room to another while his children slept and while his wife, pretending to snore peacefully, observed him with one eye open. In the living room he sat in front of the piano, arms crossed, glaring at it intently, until the anger that filled him became unbearable. He felt betrayed—but by whom?—and even that he'd fallen into a trap—but set by whom? He ended up pulling his clothes back on to rove around in the middle of the night, while scrupulously avoiding the jazz bars. What was running through his mind? Marguerite, with her face as perfect as the Virgin Mary's? Or her long white fingers, which, it appeared, he wanted so much to caress? Was he dying to ask her advice, she who was so clairvoyant?

One particularly grey afternoon, while his wife was breastfeeding the baby in the kitchen, he went into the room and sat himself in front of the door to the alleyway, as if to bear witness to the dying day. In a zombie-like voice, he told her that he was going to send all his employers packing. But why? she asked him. What had happened to him? Why did he refuse to talk to her, his comrade in arms? If you could believe Oscar's sisters, he looked at her with compassion, and might even have asked himself if he'd not senselessly underestimated her. Oh, nothing has any importance anymore, he said. And what are we going to live on now? she exclaimed. After a long silence, he turned about and resumed his wanderings through the neighbourhood.

One day, as he was roaming around the port, mesmerized by the gulls performing their spiralling trajectories against a backdrop of puffed-up cumulus, he happened on a demonstration where hundreds of strikers were brandishing placards and banners, and chanting slogans he had never before heard: No to paupers' salaries! For human working conditions! Duplessis, enemy of the workers! No to the Padlock Law! Suddenly, a man broke away from the demonstrators to rush towards him. What are you doing here? asked Chester, who, faced with his silence, told him about the picket line, whose purpose was to support the metalworker comrades who were threatened with massive layoffs. And you, what's happening with you, O.P.? Look at you, said Chester, worriedly taking in his haggard appearance, his straggly beard, and the mud-stained clothes he'd been wearing for weeks. What did I tell you, eh? You can't trust the capitalists, they'll always screw you in the end. When invited to take part in the demonstration, Oscar replied that his heart wasn't in it. Unity is strength, when are you going to understand that, O. P.? Faced with Oscar's lack of enthusiasm, Chester asked him about his financial situation. In a neutral tone, as if he were talking about someone else's life, he confessed that he'd exhausted his savings, that his little family was now making do thanks to Beverly's father, a man who, even when he was working, had no particular affection for him, but who now felt free to mock him in front of everyone. When Chester suggested that he find work as a docker, he was silent for a good while, looking about him, then half-heartedly nodded his head. Why did he accept the offer? Did he feel that he'd sunk so low that he had nothing more to lose? Or that he could at last drown his sorrows in fatigue and live in peace, with no dreams or illusions? Whatever the case, Chester arranged to meet him in the port the next day before joining the demonstration.

Two days later, Oscar began working at night. He filled crates in the hold of a cargo ship. As he might go down and climb back up as many as a hundred times a day, he left the port depleted in the cool light of morning, just as the city was waking and its citizenry was flowing in the opposite direction. Once home, he didn't have the strength either to talk or to take a shower, and he just lay down fully clothed. Beverly disapproved and reprimanded him, but he only heard a few words before falling asleep. This routine suited him: he couldn't bear to think back on his former artistic ambitions, and even less on his dreams of grandeur, which he now saw as storybook fantasies.

When his old neighbourhood friends ran into him and asked how things were going, O.P. walked on without replying, as if he'd gone deaf. *Bloodseed*, did you see the zombie face on him? Has he broken with his lovely wife? Or with his father, a puzzle if there ever was one, always sitting on the front steps of his house, with his death mask? Is it true what they say? Did he have a falling out with the buxom wife of the Twilight Station's owner? What? Did fate strike him a blow, as some of the neighbourhood's elders thought? It's said that every morning he hoped with all his heart to have changed his life, but amidst the familiar shapes of the furniture in his room, what loomed up before him straightaway was the puffy, bristled face of Art T., just like on his record covers, one eye closed, the other half shut, the mouth disdainful and always agape, as if caught in mid-breath. Despite himself, he heard again his rival's head-long musical phrases, the bursts of machine gun fire, the deranged carousel. Were the gossipmongers right to claim that Oscar was even, the ultimate sacrilege, questioning his faith? In any case, rumour had it that he resented God for having played a double game, tell-ing him one thing through the preacher's voice and the opposite the following day.

One day at noon, knowing that his mother wasn't working, he stopped by his parents'. After having greeted him with a kiss, and as she was turning back to her stove, Davina declared: So it's true what they say, my boy, you look like a ghost. Despite Oscar's objec-tions, she poured into a bowl a chicken stock she'd pre-pared the day before, diced up in a flash a carrot and a pumpkin, garnished it all with a bunch of coriander, and heightened the soup's flavour with a strong pepper purée she put together every Sunday after church. True to her habits, she was content just to sit in front of her son and watch him eat; after a while, she asked him if it was true what she'd heard, that he wasn't giving shows anymore? That he was working as a docker? She acknowledged his sense of responsibility; a man, a real man, did whatever it took to feed his family.

To her mind, times were tough for everyone, espe-cially in this part of the world, where the *Chef* con-trolled everything. Although she was a proud believer, she wasn't stupid; in any case, she was smart enough to see that the Church was too often seduced by the smell of money. As for their community, everyone was convinced that they were on the same side as the English Canadians. There, she gave a little laugh followed by a sucking noise: If they could only take a look at how they treat us, they wouldn't come out with such rubbish. She sighed and, in conclusion, said dreamily and without self-pity: The cows out front always get the clean water. Soon, as she began talking to herself again, it's said that Oscar, not without remorse, began to wonder whether his mother's delirium was not due to his abandoning the piano. He took hold of her and looked her straight in the eye: *Mudda*, I need you to read my hand. A sly smile appeared on Davina's lips, and she studied Oscar's left hand, because as everyone knows, that's the one that tells the future for right-handed men. She mumbled some gibberish, closed her eyes, opened them several times as if to spy on Oscar, declared imperiously that his mental landscape was far too murky, but wait, it's getting clearer. I see an uneven future, you're smiling widely, but your lower lip is trembling with cold and unease, you're afraid of a shadow that's grazing the walls of your house. Whose shadow is it? he asked. Davina leaned in closer to her son's hand before finally shrugging her shoulders, letting her own hand drop, and resuming her dialogue with the voices that haunted her. Oscar asked himself what he was doing there. Did he doubt, if only for an instant, his mother's powers? He got up, leaned down to plant a kiss on her brow, and left.

According to a number of witnesses, he began again to roam around like a pariah. Now he walked with a sense of purpose, stepping with determination, as if seeking to die of exhaustion. He stalked all the neighbourhood's streets, all its alleyways, all its parks, crossed all its intersections in every direction possible and, if need be, against red lights. At dawn, a few people saw him heading down towards the canal, where he was soon wrapped in the arms of a thick fog, God's breath, always conducive to reflection, and that brings us back to the beginning of our story. He leaned on the railing bordering the canal to take in the sinister vista where a forest of assorted chimneys was fuming away and where garbage was strewn over water as leaden as the air. A short time later he climbed over the railing, his coat pockets, according to some, filled with stones. He fixed his eyes on the waves, as if his gaze could pierce straight through to the bottom of the water. At that moment, so it was said, he had a look on his face that went beyond suffering.

Just as he was collecting himself to leap, feet together, into the canal and to say farewell to this wretched world, just as he was mustering the resolve to turn his back on life and to obey the siren call of death, a shadow stretched itself out on the ground beside his own. Too absorbed in his own suffering, Oscar didn't even turn his head towards this restless being who, in a bewildering tango, edged towards him only to back away, making him think that it was probably a stray dog. But suddenly the shadow that he'd taken for a canine turned into a very human silhouette. Still, at that precise moment, perhaps because of the storm raging in his heart, Oscar did not choose to turn in its direction. Only after many seconds did he glance that way out of the corner of his eye, seconds during which, we must believe, he realized that he didn't have the courage to jump. What he saw was a slender silhouette, dressed in an elegantly cut black raincoat and a fedora that was just as black, from which there drifted a languid plume of smoke, like an adorning feather veiling the entire face.

It's likely that the aforementioned silhouette began by asking him, in a deep but relaxed voice: How is it that the sky is so low today, as if it were going to fall on our heads? In all probability, Oscar gave no answer. This weather has lasted for days, the silhouette observed, lifting his eyes to the sky before taking a long puff on his cigarette. Is that when the man, whose face was still swathed in the vaporous cloud rising from beneath his headgear, called him by name? Some say that Oscar recoiled; others believe that he did nothing, since so many people knew him. What's certain is that just as Oscar lifted his head, more as a reflex than to see if the man spoke the truth, the ashen heavens magically transformed themselves into a cloudless sky aglow with a light that was close to summery. It would seem that only then did Oscar become fully aware of the man's presence.

He was a jazz impresario from Los Angeles who was passing through town to supervise the tour of some of his musicians. He didn't say "musicians I'm taking care of," or "the musicians I'm working with." He said, quite simply, "my musicians," which might have tipped Oscar off. Now it seems that initially he took this possessive form as a mark of affection, a sign that this man treated the artists as members of his family. A few months earlier, the impresario went on, as he was leaving Montreal in a taxi for the airport, he'd heard a brilliant pianist on the radio and asked the driver who he was. The driver didn't know, but informed him that it was a concert being broadcast directly from the Twilight Station Bar. The impresario told him to turn around and make straight for the bar in question. He described all this to Oscar in a velvety voice, and sometimes interrupted his sentences to take a puff from his cigarette or give free rein to his luminous smile, now that Oscar could make out his face. Attentive to every note, the man had listened to the rest of the performance, leaning against the bar at the back of the room, extremely impressed but, if all were to be said—because he wanted to start off on the right foot—convinced that his playing had yet to mature like a wine that's robust but well-balanced. And then, just the previous day, he'd acquired his record to discover, to his great delight, a clear improvement, even if some adjustments would be desirable, which they could talk about when the time came. He'd been looking for him all day, until the owner of the Twilight Station told him that he hadn't been performing for months. As a last resort, he'd gone for a stroll in his neighbourhood, and he'd talked to some boys he'd met in a park, who'd told him that Oscar was not doing well, that he was struggling with his inner demons, whose exact nature they did not know. I'm catching a plane this afternoon, and I decided to try my luck this morning. And here you are.

Seeing Oscar hesitate, he pushed the issue: he didn't want to interfere in his private life, but all the same, it was too bad that such a talented musician should stop performing. What a waste, he said a bit more softly, as if just to himself. The man came closer and held out his hand to introduce himself: I'm Norman G. All are agreed that Oscar's attitude radically changed; the proof was that he turned right around. He must have recognized the name, since this was the most famous impresario in the world of jazz.

Faced with Oscar's obstinate silence, the man smiled, nodding his head and turning his back before letting drop, as if it were nothing at all: Fine, I'll leave you in peace, but what will Marguerite say when she learns the news? Oscar tilted his head, as if to ask himself if he'd really heard the question. I'm sorry? he murmured. The impresario froze in an attitude of mock anticipation, still facing away, his back straight. *Bloodseed*, who are you? said Oscar. The man slowly swivelled on his heels, approached him, and answered: I will be everything you want me to be. Some claim that to counter Oscar's dubious air, he added, with just the suggestion of a smile on his lips: Know that I am the sacred fire, but that I am also as malleable as gold. Oscar himself is of no help to us here, because in his interviews on this, as with other crucial events in his life, he chose to keep his own counsel.

Just as the morning light began sending forth enough energy for the city dwellers to at last start bustling about, a few people spotted the two men, side by side, walking away from the canal. They passed alongside warehouses and factories, and crossed a residential neighbourhood where a fifty-year-old in overalls, straight from his truck, was doling out piles of newspapers to young newsboys, and two or three, later, swore by all the gods to have caught a glimpse of them. By the time they reached the old town, Oscar was already walking with more of a spring in his step. Finally, when they entered the street of Norman G.'s hotel, they were sauntering nonchalantly, as if they were old friends who had been separated for far too long by unforeseen and unhappy circumstances. From now on this man would be Oscar's constant companion, and as such would become, from the point of view that will be ours, both his blessing and his curse.

4

The night Oscar performed at Carnegie Hall in New York, the concert was broadcast live on the CBC, where he had been working only a few months earlier. Even if most people in the neighbourhood had a radio, or at the very least a rudimentary receiver that you had to take a fist to every so often to keep it going, the rumour mill had done its work, and all you had to do was to follow the electric wire that unspooled from sidewalk to sidewalk, from street to street, fording rivulets of urine, skirting brothels where one fornicated loud and clear, bisecting the din on the jazz-club strip, and slicing right through the baseball diamond where the last holdouts were trying in vain to complete a ninth inning that refused to bite the dust—all you had to do was follow the wire leading to the set perched on the rise at the north end of the park, deposited there by Oscar's brothers and sisters, to hear, in the company of other enthusiasts, the shower of notes from the piano-playing prodigy. There were at least two hundred, perhaps three hundred souls huddled together like wasps around an upset honey pot, their ears straining to hear all the cascades and arpeggios. Not a bit nervous, he played as if he were in his parents' living room and once more twelve years old: he performed his music not only with youthful passion, but with a joyous vitality and a light touch that has always been the mark of greatness, of courtesy wed to intelligence.

Of all the pieces he played, the one that from one day to the next raised him to glorious heights was a slow swing, restrained, tinged with mischief, shot through with swoon-inducing staccatos and legatos. It was called "Tenderly." How did he manage that tour de force, transmuting piano chords into human vocal chords with such gentle grace? Bah, said the brothers and sisters to whoever asked the question, it runs in the family. Still, it was this subtle amalgam of sophistication and simplicity that won the hearts of all the music lovers in the park, such that at the end of the concert, while everyone prepared to disperse, several made a show of wiping some irritant from their eyes, powerless to hide the feelings that had welled up in them, as if Oscar had miraculously interpreted the scores of their inner lives.

Norman G.'s great innovation was to have his protégés—about fifteen of the most prominent musicians in the world of jazz—play in concert halls usually reserved for classical music, and to bring in box office receipts far exceeding the meagre sums offered by nightclubs. According to him, not only would jazz be profitable in those prestigious venues, but it would also free it from its reputation as a marginal art form promoted by a few mobsters trying to redirect their activities into music, a reputation recently enhanced thanks to the boppers, whom neither Norman nor Oscar held in very high esteem.

From the very beginning, Oscar's appearances in the United States made him rich. He was like a pirate finding a treasure on his first ocean voyage. From one day to the next, he was able to stop worrying about survival and to concentrate on his art. It's said that on rainy Sunday mornings, when he looked back on the turbulent days when he wanted to drown his sorrows in the canal, he couldn't believe that he was really this man who saw his reflected image in the filthy water. Unbeknownst to his father, he provided for his parents, slipping wads of bills into envelopes that he mailed every month to his mother. When he had her on the phone, Davina assured him in a whisper—backed up with winks of the eye that she forgot he couldn't see—that she had respected to the letter his request that she talk of the money to no one, and promised on his next visit to prepare a meal he'd never forget. She neglected to tell him that she was sharing out the money to those of her children who were in need.

More importantly, everything indicated that his collaboration with Norman G. had turned Oscar's view of himself upside down. What exactly was going on in his head? Anyone who ventured an answer would have to be very shrewd. What is certain is that never again would anyone surprise him on the edge of the canal. Rather, you saw him in concert hall lobbies, dressed in a powder-blue three-piece suit, eyes sparkling, his smile as gleaming as the Chevy Bel Air Deluxe he'd just bought, while photographers blitzed him with their flash bulbs and journalists with their crafty questions. The next day you found his photo in the newspaper as he held out his hand to a theatre owner or a municipal politician, displaying an affability too radiant to be believable, especially for those who had encountered him during his weeks of distress. Who was he trying to kid, after all? Had he swept under a carpet of denial all the questionings as to his worth as an artist? And the spectre of Art T.? The neighbourhood residents could only speculate, since, what with his constant travelling, almost no one saw him. Certainly, the wound was still open, infected even, but apparently he made a huge effort to pretend that all was well in the best of all worlds: in interviews he readily praised the quality of Art T.'s music, then quickly steered the conversation towards his own musical universe, his own ambitions.

Now Oscar and Norman were as tight as a ring on a finger. If by chance you entered a luxurious hotel in Los Angeles, you would not have been surprised to see them talking into the wee hours while a waiter or barmaid, suppressing a yawn, refilled their glasses. Or if you happened on them in the Big Apple's Central Station, it would have been poor form to stare at them wide-eyed as they were buying fares at the ticket window for some unknown destination. And if by chance you passed in front of a famous Chicago restaurant, you wouldn't have batted an eyelid on seeing them cheek by jowl, because Norman was now his alter ego, his inner voice—a voice not to be trusted, if you hearkened to what some bad-mouthers said in private.

The world of jazz was divided on the subject of Norman G. Some praised his business acumen and his civility, qualities that had opened doors to spheres of influence hitherto deemed inaccessible, enabling him to build a sprawling empire, both an artists' agency and a record company; others described him as a man consumed by society life and as a compulsive initiator of huge parties that almost always degenerated into orgies and ended badly, with him as host taking offence at some trifle—a word out of place, a bad joke—and unceremoniously throwing his guests into the street. The first group swore by the genuineness of his charm, a sign of his big heartedness; the second described a per-fidious individual, pathologically resentful, who relied on his charisma to tyrannize those close to him and ulti-mately to bleed them dry.

It would seem that Oscar didn't know where he stood with him, which explains why, when they agreed to meet in a social setting and he spotted his impresario in the midst of the guests, he eyed him from afar. Was he trying to get to the bottom of his furtive smiles? His strange way of dipping his head when he turned away from someone? His oratorical gifts when addressing a small group of five or six people, beside themselves with admiration? It's said that Oscar's ambivalence was such that he began to view his impresario as a smartly dressed guardian angel; because, after all, had he not kept all his promises? But just then, snatches of conversation between two people he didn't know would reach his ears, wherein Norman G. was referred to in unflattering terms: for the one, his remoteness was proof positive of his shifty nature; for the other, the treatment Norman reserved for a disloyal musician was at the very least suspicious, and there followed a sordid story involving the mafia, a smoke-filled bar, a baseball bat, and a swollen face. As Oscar was busy imagining scenes out of a film, Norman came up behind him, placed a hand on his shoulder, and asked him, with an ambivalent smile on his lips, if he was bored, then remarked, as if to intentionally provoke him: You may not yet play like Art, but all the same you're a hell of a pianist.

When Oscar went back to the neighbourhood, his old friends now limited themselves to a simple wave of the hand and kept their distance, as if they were intimidated by his sudden prosperity. During that time, according to his brothers and sisters, Davina produced enormous meals that so shocked Josué that he clung to her skirts, notebook in hand: But where did you get the money for that mountain of crab, that crate of cod, that chicken as big as a turkey? And those pies and pastries, whose flavours he'd never even imagined? *Bloodseed*, had she robbed a bank, or what? Davina came and went from her pots to the sink, punctuating her rapid steps with her constant sucking noise as if she were chomping at the bit.

Even at his parents', he was no longer treated to intimacies such as taps on his back or on his cheek. Rather, he was prodded with questions about his fabulous life. Everyone wanted to know about the halls where he played, the celebrities he met, the cities he visited. Oscar answered patiently, in a manner new to him, which some thought steeped in false modesty. In time, the questions stopped, doubtless because the scenes he described were so remote from their daily lives that they ended up being hurtful.

In the course of those evenings, Josué spent most of his time sitting in the half-light of the living room, as still as a frozen tree, with his familiar, unwavering expression on his lips. No one knew if he expected nothing more from life, or if he were hoping that some violent event would take place to wrench him out of his silence. On each visit Oscar sat down at his side, rubbed his hands together as if lending an ear to the silence, smiled like a child as he fixed his gaze on the worn wooden floor, and at last talked about this and that. He was also trying to show that he bore him no grudge—which was only partly true, according to some—for having forced him listen to Art T. to lance the boil of his self-regard. He told all and sundry that he'd sought it out, that lesson in humility, and that now he'd turned the page. Because, seriously, why would he resent his begetter, the man who was getting by on a miserable pension, who had hidden away in a closet—was that possible?—his telescope, and spent all his days listening to records? No, he couldn't be angry with this man who had endured so many humiliations in order to support his family; and on taking his leave he leaned down to plant a loud kiss on his father's brow, as one would for an infant.

In the narrow hall, before he left, someone always cornered him to ask about his mysterious impresario. Why did he never come to town? They'd soon start thinking that he was snubbing them. A sardonic smile on his lips, Chester, who never missed an opportunity to goad his brother, said: Maybe it's you who's ashamed of your family, O.P.? Now Oscar—besides his eternal gratitude to his brother for having found him a job when everything in his life was going from bad to worse—had matured, and could no longer be unsettled for so little. Yes, that's it, day and night I'm tortured by this secret shame; that's why even when I'm at the other end of the United States, I do all I can to come back here on Friday nights, just to be bored by your company. Everyone laughed, after which Chester, tamed, challenged him in a more conciliatory tone: Okay, *bredda*, but you're going to have to show him to us, your impresario, or we'll start believing you've made him up. Oscar raised his arms with his hands spread wide, an evasive smile on his lips: the moment was fast approaching, he could tell.

One Friday night, while the men were rubbing their hands together over the coal stove, and the cold was etching dramatic patterns into the window panes, Davina, her nose buried in her pots—so deep that her face was lost in steam—asked Oscar if his impresario knew anything at all about how to live, because a true gentleman would move heaven and earth to meet his protégé's family. It was the least he could do, to show them the simple courtesy of honouring with his presence his favourite pianist's flesh and blood. She added, not without irony, but addressing no one in particular, that in that way he could kill two birds with one stone, and reassure himself, God help us, that he wasn't getting mixed up with the lowest of the low, with some scheming profiteers. Oscar was just starting to tie himself up in knots, explaining that West Indian customs were not the same as North American ones, when a silhouette materialized on the doorstep, projecting its shadow into the kitchen. All heads turned, including that of Davina, who burned her index finger in the callaloo soup. I'm in complete agreement with you, Davina, said the voice of Norman G., as smooth as eternity. He advanced into the middle of the kitchen and tugged methodically on each of his fingers to remove his leather gloves. A man such as you describe would indeed not be worthy to be called a gentleman. He ceremoniously doffed his fedora and his coat, which he carefully folded before draping it over his forearm. That done, Davina discreetly elbowed Prudence, who hastened to relieve the new arrival of his personal belongings, depositing them on the bed in the master bedroom.

After the formal introductions, he installed himself like a simple mortal in a wicker chair, complimented Davina on her soup with a brio that drew nervous smiles, and took the time to talk with everyone in turn, as if he truly shared their preoccupations. He listened with undivided attention to the trials of Oscar's younger sister at the textile factory, making it seem as though her fragmented anecdotes truly touched him. Like the others, he exclaimed when Davina raised the lid of the cooking pot where there lay a trout in coconut milk with pineapple, and later, when he declared his love for their native island, which he knew like the back of his hand, he said, from having often spent time there, as much for vacations as for business, they all melted like snow in the sun. When Davina learned that he knew her former neighbours on the island, she rose up, pushed back her chair in a rush of enthusiasm that left Oscar gasping, and, giddy with joy, almost fell into the arms of the impresario, who had also risen to his feet.

Once he was gone and all the others in bed, sedated by the lavish meal, it's said that Davina found herself alone with Oscar in the half light of the kitchen, where the earlier exchanges still resonated amid a deafening silence. He's an extraordinarily charming man, she said, but when he moves from one room to another, the flowers fade and a scent of sulphur is left behind. I had to spray the house with a tincture of gardenia. Oscar's eyes widened, and Davina rose to hang up the pots on a rack fashioned from coat hangers. Her back turned, she said: Don't be naïve, my son. The devil is everywhere; like dirt, he wants to spread himself over everything. That's the way it's always been, and what can you do about it, eh? She turned towards him and shrugged her shoulders. The best you can do is to keep him close and manage him. Oscar kept silent as if he were thinking deeply, and in a hesitant voice he asked her if she was certain of what she was saying. As certain as when I met your father for the first time, and I knew that, whatever I did, we were going to be wed. Of course, replied Oscar, but to have peace it's best to chase the devil away, no? She shook her head, before discharging a sucking noise from between her incisors. You'd be making a big mistake. She snapped her fingers. You can't get rid of the devil just like that. Whether we like it or not, he's right there, following us like a shadow, ready to pounce as soon as we make a wrong move. As for you, be on your guard, he loves to show himself when you're on the road to success, she said, talking like someone who speaks the truth. Then she hung another pot on the rack.

A week later, before going away on tour, while Oscar was down on all floors in the living room playing with his eldest son, less for pleasure than to be pardoned by Beverly for his frequent absences, the telephone rang. At the other end of the line, the unctuous voice of Norman G. reminded him that he was a man of his word, suggested that he give a listen to the public radio station, then hung up without saying goodbye. When Oscar turned on the radio, as his son was busy building a structure with connectable bricks, a commercial was vaunting the virtues of a dish soap. Soon, a host introduced a classical piano competition featuring the music of Franz Liszt. If the first entrant left him cold, his heart leapt when he heard the second, because he recognized instantly her delicate touch, unparalleled. He was overcome by a surge of emotion so intense that he saw himself again behind hospital walls on the brink of death, when a pale young girl entered his life like a gift from divine providence. God in heaven, was it possible? Marguerite played here and there a few false notes which, with a lover's ardour, he quickly forgave.

As soon as she'd finished her piece, Oscar dressed as fast as if the house were on fire, and rushed past Beverly, who, in her dressing gown, was breastfeeding the baby. Where was he going? she asked in a curt voice. He had to go to the radio studio, he'd forgotten his scores. Then he invented an unlikely story, which unfolded with less and less conviction the longer it got. Seeing that he was becoming entangled in a web of lies, he shut the door softly behind him without finishing his last sentence. Once on a main road, Oscar hailed a taxi and sped towards the CBC. In the back seat he was feverish with emotion, and kept tugging at his shirt collar. When he arrived in front of the broadcast building, a plump young woman was just coming out, and they found themselves face to face. He stared at her for a long time. Behind her adult and admittedly portly features, he desperately sought traces of the Marguerite he had known; it was as if a surfeit of skin had been hastily applied to the slender young girl of the past. Her name was Marguerite, was it not? She nodded her head in a gesture he thought reflected her elegance and timidity. Was it really her? How to be sure? Did he suspect a plot on Norman's part? Was he already suspicious of his impresario? In any case it seemed that he had a great need to believe it was her, because he told her that, despite the time that had passed, she hadn't changed, that she was as ravishing as in his dreams, where over and over he encountered her by chance in the streets of an imagined city. She seemed taken aback at first, as if she were passing in swift review all the men she'd met in the course of her life, but when he approached her to take her in his arms, she consented to wrap hers around him as well.

They walked together side by side, despite the angry winter pushing snow down towards the river. He bared his soul to her, and she threw him timid glances, as if trying to recognize this man who was treating her with such reverence, or simply to persuade herself that he was not deceiving her. By common consent, they went into a diner; in front of the smoked meat sandwiches they squeezed each others' hands as if they were lemons. His voice breaking, he confessed that his treasured memory of her in the hospital had given him strength, had helped him to hold his course during all those years. When she asked him to name the hospital in question, Oscar stiffened, and his eyebrows flew up; she hastened to remind him of how young she had then been, how the time she'd spent there had been shorter than his, and that she'd suffered lapses of memory due to her illness. He seemed reassured and promised never again to leave her.

At the start of their relationship, as she still lived with her parents, she had to lie about Oscar's identity so that they wouldn't forbid her from leaving the house. People's thinking changed at a snail's pace, you had to arm yourself with patience, she cautioned Oscar. After a few weeks she saw that she was correct to bank on Oscar's celebrity, and her parents finally allowed her, grudgingly, to see him, especially when she told them about his earnings and the influential people in his entourage. She didn't tell them that he was married. Sometimes she didn't appear. It seemed that she suffered from a mysterious illness that left her fatigued for no reason: she was out of breath after climbing three stairs and coughed compulsively on the first warm days, when the city was overrun by the seed-bearing tufts of weeds.

Soon they were seeing each other every day, and dared to spend the night together, first just to talk, then at last to unite in a communion of caresses, of archings and churnings that soon had them war-weary, what with their uncertain health. Oscar was floating on air, persuaded, as he confided to one of his sisters, that he'd rediscovered his lost love. They began to spend weekend mornings in bed, Marguerite's head resting on Oscar's chest as he sketched out future projects for the two of them, and she listened, giving her assent from time to time, as if she were really saying to him, "Why not." He was living some of the happiest days of his life, even if he never expressed himself that way to those close to him. He told his confidants that the only fly in the ointment was Beverly, who did all she could to make his life difficult: she constantly sniffed his shirts, phoned the members of his new trio behind his back to ask about who he was seeing, and burst into tears when she found, while searching through his jacket pockets, the bill from a fancy restaurant.

From that point on, Oscar and Marguerite were inseparable, because even when he went on tour, she went with him. Musically, he began a period of intense experimentation, in the course of which he discovered, after much trial and error, that a trio consisting of piano, double bass, and electric guitar best suited his personality and artistic ambitions. It provided him with the creative intimacy of reduced ensembles so dear to the boppers, it opened him up to modernity thanks to the electric guitar, and it ensured—without drums—a rhythmic suppleness at all times, forcing himself to cultivate a sustained, dominant pianistic style. His involvement with Norman G. enabled him to rub shoulders with many accomplished musicians before settling on Ray B. and Herb E., both Americans, the first of West Indian background himself, the second from a white southern family—all of which pleased him, since it made him feel as if he were making a strong political gesture, an affirmation of coexistence, in music as in life. The group matured quickly, achieving such unity, such perfection in the art of swing, that some critics claimed that the three musicians had been launched into the world by God with the sole purpose of coming together one day. Before long jazz fans all over the globe were dubbing the group "the best trio in the world." And for good reason, because to experience one of their concerts was to follow a spellbinding exchange between the assured and teasing discourse of the piano, the constant, supportive murmur of the double bass, and the sprightly exclamations and ecstatic sighs of the guitar.

As they spent most of their time together, on tour or not, the three musicians developed very close ties. Just as it was on stage, each had access to the thoughts of the two others, whether they were existential ponderings, elusive moods hard to pin down, or simply the memory of a good joke heard the day before, and often they burst out laughing without a single word being spoken. It was a surprising phenomenon, but when you took a closer look you saw that it was all in the order of things, since, as Ray said in an interview, they spent more time together than with their wives.

It's said that, on a particularly hot night, in the shadow of magnolias, talking together on the terrace of a hotel in the United States, Oscar thanked Norman for a gesture he'd made: he'd stood up to the owner of a hall who insisted that whites be placed in the even-numbered seats, and the blacks in the odd, as was the custom in those parts. Despite the guns, the chains, the baseball bats, and the avalanche of insults from some rednecks, Norman stood firm, thanks to the complicity of the police, whose higher-ups he'd brought onside, thanks to some generous bribes. The impresario shrugged his shoulders, and this apparent indifference made a big impression on Oscar, who right then began pondering, as he confessed to those close to him, what the scandalmongers were bruiting about concerning Norman: that his antiracist campaign was all a sham, since he was interested in, and guided by, nothing more than his lust for money. After a moment, Norman gestured to him to come closer and murmured in his ear that, in a collaboration like theirs, everyone had to do his part. It seems that, although he knew what he was implying, Oscar asked him to be more precise. Norman sat back in his chair, tilted his hat back on his head, and looked around him again so that all the lights from the streetlamps were reflected in his gaze. Have I not kept my word? he asked, in a voice as mellifluous as the note from an oboe. Did you not get everything you wanted? O.P. nodded with a frightened air, after which Norman mumbled a sentence whose last words, it appears, are the only ones he understood: Art T. If the ogre, as you call him, is in our line of sight, we'll never reach the top, right? Oscar didn't assent right away, too preoccupied, it seems, remembering a saying that was a favourite of his mother's: the cat steps differently when he wants to catch a rat.

5

It was about that time when Oscar, it appears, began to have a dream about running into Art T. leaning at a bar alone, mum as a frog, his gaze focused obstinately on the beer in front of him, totally indifferent to the revolver being pointed directly at him. Invariably, O.P. ended up panicking, his heart loud in his chest and perspiration coursing down his cheeks. When he fired point blank, Art did not crumble, he just sat there as if nothing had happened and didn't even deign to look his way. In another dream, Oscar was walking on a bridge, large stretches of which were hidden in thick fog. When he met Art by chance, he went up to him and tried in vain to throw him into the water below. Every nightmare left him starting upright in bed, all in a sweat, panting as if he'd just run a hundred yard dash. Marguerite, waking, asked him if everything was all right. A bad actor, he said of course, I'm fine, and turned his back.

One night, when Oscar was rehearsing in a Manhattan bar, it's said that a young man came to tell him that the great Bud P., who defined bebop piano at that time, was playing a stone's throw away at another bar and that he'd be more than honoured if Oscar were to sit in on his show. Ordinarily, after each performance, Oscar wanted only one thing: to go and find Marguerite under the hotel room bedcovers to breathe in the aroma of dark, wet spruce that emanated from her recurring dreams. However, so as not to offend this fellow musician, who was known for his extreme sensitivity, he decided, it seems, to find his way to the bar in question, if only for half an hour, and to make his presence felt. The room, smaller and darker than that where he himself performed, was packed with enthusiasts spellbound by Bud's energetic, dissonant, and angry playing. Oscar sat down at the very back and ordered a soft drink. When Bud spotted him out of the corner of his eye, he asked the public to warmly applaud the fabulous pianist who was honouring them with his presence, and he dedicated his next piece to him, which inspired Oscar to raise a glass to his health.

His playing soon had Oscar deeply perplexed. Was he mistaken, or was Bud embarking on a long introduction to "Tenderly," the piece everyone identified with Oscar ever since the beginning of his career? Was it, again, his imagination that was playing tricks on him, or was Bud now mimicking his all-powerful left hand, his wry touch, and his impetuous runs up and down the scale? When he heard Bud's first chuckle, then those of his followers—even more wounding—he had the awful feeling that his ears had begun to bleed. After a few measures, certain now that this fool was having him on, Oscar rose and left. He wandered into the night, where every vehicle that passed seemed bent on attacking him personally. How to respond to such an affront, *rawtid*? In the end—and perhaps that's what he found hard to grasp—it's written in the stars that sooner or later someone will pave the way for the envious and the indolent who look at hard-won success and choose to call it "luck."

That night, he woke Marguerite to spill out everything that was weighing on his heart. When his mistress advised him, between two yawns, to forget that story, not to take it so seriously, because there were jealous people everywhere and there always would be, he felt that his suffering left her cold, and he got up and slammed the door to go and join Norman G. at the hotel bar. The incident with Bud P. seemed to amuse his impresario, who, without being aware of it, concurred with Marguerite: he had not seen the last of that envy-ridden clique. With this foul bog of rancour still brewing inside him, Oscar launched into a diatribe against Bud P. and his music, snatches of which were overheard by several late-night drinkers. They claim that O.P.'s rage drew gales of laughter from Norman, who in response, told him what he knew about that strange individual: that he was unstable, and into drugs up to his ears. A scrapper, he broke with everybody, always over trifles; he was an egoistic monster, a lunatic. Norman patted Oscar's hand and told him not to worry, he'd take care of it. And on that note, he ordered two more whiskeys on the rocks.

A few days later, after a show, he was told that Miles D., a trumpet player very much in vogue, had that very day declared on the radio, at an hour when there was a large listening public, that Oscar clearly had a lot to learn about the blues. He was not from the United States, where jazz was born, that much was obvious. What was more, he plagiarized just about everyone in sight, had no originality, and was bone lazy. As Oscar sank into a state of bitter despondency, Ray and Herb urged him to ignore the spiteful remarks; but that was easier said than done, because, to all appearances, Miles D.'s words echoed constantly in his head. Back in his hotel room he told all this to Marguerite, but she, not daring to say anything now for fear that he would explode, just answered in monosyllables, which Oscar took for indifference, and he slammed the door again, this time to go and take the air. While a mean wind was heralding the imminent arrival of winter, he brooded and reflected on a human nature abruptly revealed to him in all its shabby spitefulness. From this point on, a favourite strategy of those who wanted to denigrate his music was to espouse the trumpeter's argument that he had no roots in jazz, ignoring all those whom old Jackson always ordered us to remember: the West Indians who helped invent this divine music in the American South early in the century.

It's said that a few months later, as he was sipping his coffee at home and leafing through the paper, Oscar choked and sprayed brown liquid onto his shirtsleeves and into his wife's face on learning that Bud P., the mad pianist, had just died of tuberculosis. As Beverly was swabbing herself off with a towel, Oscar recalled, not without remorse, his impresario's words, declaring that he would "take care of" Bud. As his wife tried to hold back her tears, he found himself wondering—while unconsciously smearing jam on his face with his fingers—what power this man had. *Bloodseed*, was his mother right about him? It wasn't the first time he'd noted such a coincidence, he'd already heard about the disappearance of three people who'd had differences with Norman G. In all cases, the authorities found their bodies only months later, one in a dump, one in a rocky riverbed, and one in an obscure alleyway in a sordid Chicago neighbourhood. It was said that two of the victims had not long before injected themselves with dope that some mysterious and providential soul had left on their doorsteps.

Meanwhile, every time he came back to Montreal, Oscar confessed to his friends that the city was a bit more unrecognizable. The new mayor had initiated a "big clean-up," as the papers called it, and he was targeting the jazz bars, with their share of bootleggers, pimps, and bookmakers. Just one stroll was enough for Oscar to see the changes underway; not only were the bars closing, but they were being replaced by clubs where francophone *chansonniers* performed, such as the one he came across one night, a dignified gentleman with a scarf around his neck, strumming his guitar, and singing about a driverless train speeding northwards. And the papers were saying that the French Canadians were organizing to try to free whole sections of the population from poverty, under the inscrutable gaze of the old *Chef*, who—and here, the papers were silent—on the one hand blew on the embers of nationalism in his fiery speeches, and on the other made dubious deals with English Canadian businessmen and the priests.

Norman G. didn't at all like the idea that French Canadians might hold the reins of power and urged Oscar to move to Toronto, a city, he argued, that was not burdened with the French language, where the jazz scene was expanding, and where, no small thing, money grew on trees. Was the decision as easy to make as it seemed? Was he not sensitive to the obvious sorrow in the family at the prospect of his leaving? Did he wonder if he'd be able to go on creating there with the same energy? Probably he dismissed those considerations with the back of his hand, since he already saw himself as a rocket that was steadily drawing away from the earth, one whose momentum, for the moment, had something exhilarating about it. Besides, as he had long since acquired the habit of throwing himself into his work to forget his cares, one might conclude that that is exactly what he did. He moved his little family into a wealthy Toronto suburb while secretly renting an apartment downtown for Marguerite. Beverly, who suspected what was going on behind her back, was no longer reluctant to say things as she saw them: I know that the faithful wife wears the worn clothes, O.P., I'm not dumb.

One winter night, during his last number in a Washington bar, he was fighting off sleep, the sweat was coursing down his temples and onto the keyboard drop by drop, his fingers were sliding around, and false notes kept intruding into his playing. It was one of those days when he wasn't comfortable and when his music held no magic, as he confessed to his friends. While the public, which you had to believe was being rocked to sleep as well, was applauding without much enthusiasm, Ray gestured with his head so he'd look towards the bar's front door. When Oscar saw the misshapen, ogre-like silhouette, he ventured, it seems, a tired smile. For months he'd been accepting all invitations to play in Washington and Los Angeles, the two cities where Art T. appeared most often.

When the show was over he joined Art, who was there with his distinctive, involuntary grimace, just like in the photos, sitting at the bar in front of a glass of beer with an ample head, exactly as in Oscar's dreams. The ogre vigorously shook his hand and gave him a falsely nonchalant embrace, as if they already knew each other. Oscar played better when he was falling asleep, Art said to him, because then the unconscious, that devil, threw reason to the winds. But he shouldn't try to dethrone him, he was the king, and if he had to fight bare knuckle to defend his title, he wouldn't hesitate for a second. At these words, Oscar went cold, while Art contorted with laughter. The barman followed suit, as did all the other drinkers around, after which Oscar had no choice but to join in the collective hilarity. According to what he confided to one of his friends, Art was worse than he'd imagined him: he was a monster of vanity, plagued by a competitive urge that he barely bothered to camouflage behind a gruff, brash facade.

As soon as Oscar offered an opinion on a city or a fellow musician, Art took a large swig of beer and cut him off, as if he found what he had to say inexpressibly tedious. When Art paused for breath, Oscar chanced a look, and each time Art was glaring at him, as if to say that despite his blindness, he too still had an eye. It has to be said that Art—this was well known—tended to associate courtesy with honesty, viewing the former as the source of the second, and demanding that everyone respect it, with the notable exception of himself. And when Art asked if he wanted to continue the discussion elsewhere, O.P. didn't hesitate to say yes. Was he respecting to the letter the well-known adage dear to Norman G.'s heart, which stipulated that you had to keep your friends close to you and your enemies even closer?

The party took place in a neighbourhood populated exclusively by *breddas*, and in fact, Oscar saw nothing but *breddas* in the vast, dimly lit apartment. It seemed to be a crowd made up primarily of artists, who, after their shows, came to chat over a beer and ribs grilled on a back balcony barbecue by a cook who, in spite of the bitter cold, was dressed only in overalls. After lifting the needle off the turntable, Art announced, while massaging Oscar's neck, that here in his company was a young man who had come to fame by interpreting almost all the pieces that had brought glory to himself ten years earlier. But not to worry, he'd long since chalked it all up to inexperience and forgiven the offence, a remark that elicited scattered laughter. The young man, he went on, was a marvellous pianist who was now going to show them what he was made of. There followed a burst of applause, after which Oscar, once again, had no choice but to approach the piano and attack the keys at a furious pace, because in these duels the whole point was to make an impression. Except that he felt like he was playing in a vacuum, spitting into the wind, and his music's magic didn't function, especially since he was being assailed by Art's potent breath, with its smell of garlic, alcohol, and tobacco.

Soon, Art nudged his hip, sat himself down on the bench beside him, and added his own melodic bass line, instantly animating the guests gathered round. When Oscar ceded the entire keyboard to Art, his vigorous playing released liberating cries, joyously incredulous laughter, and applause that bit by bit modulated into an orgy of whistles and exclamations. After a while the apartment became such a carnival scene that Oscar, if you could believe what he later said, saw, as he cast his eyes around, that all the celebrants were now sporting brightly coloured clothes. *Bloodseed*, had the ogre planned all that? Were all these people part of a plot to lure him into this trap? When Art finished his piece and passed his hand through Oscar's hair, he waited quietly on the bench hoping for a tap on the shoulder—which never came—to tip him off that the whole sequence of events had been arranged in advance.

In his interviews, Oscar avoided any hint of a conflict with his rival, but various confessions he made to those close to him lead one to believe that this episode had him questioning himself for weeks. If it was clear that his music was grounded in a technique superior to that of Art T., it was nevertheless more sober and restrained. Art's playing bore the mark of raw authenticity, and his own, a studied beauty that was in some sense artificial. During a breakfast in one of the rare diners in the South open to blacks as well as whites, Ray and Herb, for all their reassurances regarding the quality of his improvisations, could not make him back down: compared to his music, that of the ogre seethed with life, reeked of sweat, exposed the naked man in all his stark reality. Some claimed that he deliberately overstated his own belittlement so that his collaborators would buoy him up. Whatever the case, if before meeting him Oscar disliked Art, now he despised him fully. He flipped the page when he came across a picture of him in the newspaper, he shut off the radio when it was broadcasting his music, and if festival organizers were so unwise as to suggest they play a duo together, he flew into a rage that surprised him more than anyone else. Still, one night, talking with Norman, he agreed that he should cultivate his "friendship" with Art, if only to keep abreast of his projects. It's said that in those days he often spoke to Art on the phone, conversations in the course of which he pretended to take an interest in his health, while promising, at Norman's suggestion, to send him cases of Canadian beer, whose woodsy aroma the ogre particularly fancied.

It's also said that in Norman's company Oscar underwent a change. If they found themselves in a restaurant his eyes clouded, his lips went dry, his palms dampened. And he sat on the edge of his chair, as if to prepare himself for any eventuality. When his impresario got up from the table, he immediately followed suit, often spilling a glass of water or sending a knife to the floor. Apparently, it was only Norman's presence that made him so nervous. If by chance they were in the company of other musicians and Norman was in a party mood, he ordered bottle after bottle of champagne, with Oscar eyeing him closely.

Often, tired of being always on his guard, Oscar's tongue loosened, and he described the excessive workload his tours demanded of him, with their burden of afternoon and evening shows, not counting the Spartan exercises he always imposed on himself in the mornings. He may have exaggerated somewhat, inventing scenes whose lead player was an intransigent bar owner, unforeseen snowstorms that prevented him from arriving on time for a show, and sleepless nights due to exhaustion. While the other musicians kept their peace, watching closely for Norman's reaction, the man in question gazed about him wearily as if waiting for Oscar to spare him and be done with this nonsense, as was his wont with "his musicians." Oscar sometimes ventured, in conclusion, that the afternoon shows were a bit much, no? While the others waited for the man to lay into him, Norman just studied him for a long time from behind the lazy spirals of his cigarette smoke and entertained his suggestions with an interest that drew chuckles from the others, but of course, in the days that followed, brought no alteration to O.P.'s schedule.

Which is why in time Oscar became more withdrawn and mistrustful. You go with dogs and you get fleas, said his detractors. Especially since it was a millionaire, and even worse, an American. Oscar's admirers claimed that no, as it was with everyone, maturity brought with it a certain vigilance, that was all.

It was then that, weary at last of the pretence, Oscar decided to level with Beverly, and he confessed straight out that he'd had a mistress for years, with whom he now wanted to live openly. Beverly reacted with remarkable stoicism; she asked him only to continue to attend to her needs and those of the children. Oscar consented at once, doubtless relieved to be absolved of his feelings of guilt in exchange for an allowance, and the discussion ended with an embrace. His detractors, who noted that on that day he left home whistling, saw in his behaviour the influence of his impresario.

Meanwhile, Norman was hounding him to produce ever more, and Oscar was unable to protest, since, despite his suspicions, he had confidence in Norman's management of his career. Besides, beset from the outset by the fear of running short of money, doubtless inherited from his begetter, and even though his bank account was being flooded with cash at the speed of a rising tide, he looked very kindly on the dizzying proliferation of records in his catalogue. That year he had to plan for the recording of six albums, the consequence being that on arriving home, his nerves strained to the limit, he barked at Marguerite if she made the slightest noise while he was rehearsing at the piano. Immediately afterwards he mumbled an apology, and she forgave him, but the harm was done, and the flickerings of fear deep in her eyes distressed him, so much so that when she took her turn at the piano, although he was terribly exasperated, her lack of talent being so plain to see, he tried to persuade himself that the melodies she played were supremely inventive.

He determined to purchase a house where they would have more space, a decision she supported. After a few months, more to satisfy the demands of their respective parents than because they wanted to, they decided to get married. Almost none of their childhood friends were invited; they claimed they preferred a small wedding. It's said that the left aisle of the church was occupied by Marguerite's family, and that of the right by Oscar's clan, and that this division, curiously, was maintained throughout the festivities, despite the couple's best efforts. Ironically, in his interviews as well as in private, Oscar continued to speak out in favour of mixed origins, which he advocated in life as in music. Meanwhile, Davina's response brought them some happy surprises: she never opposed his desire to divorce Beverly, and she never lectured him because he'd set his heart on a companion from another community. But as soon as the two families met, everyone froze as if a camera were being levelled at them, to the point where the exchanges could be counted on the fingers of one hand. One Friday night, as he was entering his parents' front hall, he heard Chester declare that Marguerite's family was as cold as a dog's nose, a comment that drew approving murmurs.

During this time, although in a very tentative fashion, Marguerite reproached him for his tendency to cultivate friendships only with people who might help promote his artistic career. If he understood rightly, he told his intimates, this was a veiled attack on the presumed narcissism he'd picked up from the celebrities he spent time with, a defect that in itself explained his total lack of interest in her. If he followed his wife's tortured reasoning, television, even in its early stages, nurtured this vanity that was tightening its grip on him. The proof was that when complete unknowns approached him to ask for an autograph, he willingly scribbled his name on the scrap of paper held out to him, regardless of the occasion they were celebrating or the place where they found themselves. Aren't you going too far? she sighed, knowing that she was making a mistake in speaking up, that he did not take well to criticism.

He began drinking with his colleagues after concerts, a ritual he'd rarely allowed himself up to then because he feared like the plague the stereotype of the bohemian jazzman, all the more so when he was alcoholic or a drug addict. And he began opening up more and more to his companions: he would have never thought that the woman of his dreams would be so jealous. He was astonished, really. Was he saying that two pianists couldn't live under the same roof? O.P. remained silent, staring into space, nodding his head as if seriously studying the question.

Faced with adversity, Oscar threw himself into his music with renewed zeal, and in the company of his sidekicks, Ray and Herb, he produced some of his best interpretations ever of the standards. He tempered his passion and virtuosity with increased aplomb, he gave pride of place to gravitas and restraint, he achieved a refinement rarely equalled. He sought salvation in his work, then felt the need for a different kind of support. He was surprised more than anyone to find himself drawn to the serenity of churches, places he had not visited for years. Entering his neighbourhood parish one day on impulse, he happened on a young minister in the extension to the nave, someone he didn't know from Adam but who agreed to talk with him. It seems that

Oscar did not hold back, but launched into a lengthy monologue, as tangled as it was suffused with a desperate sincerity. Was he really surrounded by people who resented him? Was he possessed by spirits, or was his wife truly jealous? For some time he'd felt like an orphan, had had the sensation that he was abandoned by all, including the Good Lord. But what had he done to Him to be spurned like this? When the reverend suggested, with a sigh, that he return twice a week for religious instruction, Oscar almost choked on his laughter: did he have any idea who he was?

It's said that one morning the telephone rang, waking him, and pulling him out of bed. It was Norman, asking him in a merry voice if he'd seen the newspaper, before hanging up without saying goodbye, as was his custom. Oscar opened the front door to pick up the paper from the mat and leafed through it. In the cultural section there was a box announcing the death of Art T. At first, not outwardly shaken by the news, there was just one thing he wanted to know: What was the cause of that sudden death, a question not dealt with in the article. He cancelled the concert he was to give that night in a Washington bar, and he flew to Los Angeles. The funeral took place under a leaden sky, in a cemetery bordered by tall palm trees whose fronds had been trimmed militarily. As Oscar was climbing the stone path, Art's widow spotted him, ran to him, and burst into tears in his arms. It appears that she was trembling uncontrollably and that she embraced him with a fervour that surprised him, as he hardly knew her. During the entire ceremony, wracked by sobs, she clung to him, dampened his shirt, blew her nose from time to time for the sake of appearances, all the while reeking of a perfume that made him feel queasy. Oscar kept silent, as was proper, but deep inside he was euphoric: now he had free rein, he was the world's greatest jazz pianist!

After the ceremony, she took him aside and told him that Art regarded him as his musical heir, if not his son, which left Oscar speechless. He was going to reply with a polite remark, but then an elderly man approached them to speak to the widow. After a moment, she explained to this retired painter that her husband's death was due to his kidneys giving out. Ah yes? said the gentleman. She informed him, in a low voice, but loud enough for Oscar to hear, that someone, she didn't know who, had recently been sending Art cases and cases of beer. Wasn't it reckless to have done that to a man who—everyone knew—had always had problems with alcohol? The painter was appalled, while Oscar was near to collapse. Choosing not to attend the funeral feast, he returned to the hotel. Was it Norman who had sent those cases of beer to Art, he wondered, since he himself had never had the courage to do so? So said his admirers. Nonsense, because it really was him who had sent off the bottles, replied his detractors. Whatever the case, it seems that he had a nightmare that night in the course of which, unlike what usually occurred in his dreams, Art turned to him, begging him not to shoot, but the gun went off on its own and the bullet entered his heart, putting an end to the ogre.

The next morning, while he was packing, he received a phone call from Prudence telling him Josué was dead.

It's said that he didn't move for several seconds, during which there echoed in his head, amplified by the passing of time, a phrase that Norman G. particularly favoured: everything is atoned for, both good and evil sooner or later have their price. Was that his impresario's way of making him pay for the mission he himself had undertaken in his place? Oscar would be there for his family, he'd be present at the funeral, he promised his sister. He went to the window, and as he looked down on the gaggle of rooftops, like staircases leading to paradise, he again saw his father, his face stricken but stoic, his porter's uniform spattered with blood, as he passed unsteadily through the door into the family home. From now on that was the picture that would return to him most often when he thought about his progenitor, the iconic image of what he did not want to become.

On a cold night at the end of autumn, a taxi dropped him off at his parents'. In the house, people were stifling their tears, sighing often, loudly blowing their noses. When Davina came towards him it seems he thought that she'd shrunk and that someone had dusted her hair with gunpowder, so much had the terrible sorrow aged her all at once. She now had a little girl's hands, slumping shoulders, and absent eyes. As he embraced her, and while his mother's reassuring odour permeated his entire body, he repeated his promise to answer to her needs for as long as she would be in this world. Shortly afterwards, he sat down in his father's chair for the first time. He let his eyes rest on all the furniture in the room, as if to fully embrace his begetter's point of view. Soon, as he was suffocating, he went out for a walk without letting anyone know. The street of clubs was so becalmed that its erstwhile energy seemed to be a legendary lie.

When he climbed the hill towards the north he didn't see the crowd of people flowing past him, but, again according to his sisters, thought only of his father, sometimes propped up in the living-room chair, sometimes sitting on the stairs leading to the house, in each case wearing the same mask that doomed him to silence. He again saw in his mind's eye, it's said, the train that on Fridays tunnelled through the night with a great groundswell of urgent exhalations, while at the same time he heard a double bass laying down the rhythm for the piece he was composing as he walked. When he came to himself he was being jostled, but he resolved to follow the fitful movement of the crowd. Scalpers called to him, sometimes in one language, sometimes in the other, and held out tickets. He refused three or four offers and continued walking towards the turn-stiles, finally grabbing a ticket offered by a young man in a checkered cap who looked tough but seemed to be doing this for the first time in his life.

Oscar took his seat among the crowd, at first more drawn to the spectators than to the hockey players warming up on the ice. A few metres down, a young man was kissing his girlfriend on the mouth while paw-ing at one of her breasts. Lower still, two girls were blowing kisses at a Habs player with slicked-back hair every time he came along the boards. He noted to his right the staccato delivery of the beer vendor, like the cry of an owl. When a couple leaned towards him to ask for an autograph, he willingly played along, replying not without pleasure to their questions: yes, he'd shared the stage with such-and-such a legend, a certain musician was just as nice as he seemed to be on TV, he was indeed preparing a new album, and, the hint of a smile on his lips, he was in no position to say whether or not he was the fastest pianist in the world, but thanks for the compliment. Soon, a dozen people were lined up on the stairs leading to his seat, armed with pencil and paper.

He didn't at all seem to be a man in mourning, according to some witnesses. But what was he to do, burst into tears in public? replied his admirers. As soon as the match began the Habs went on the offence, and at each appearance of the Rocket on the ice the crowd lifted to cheer on his canny feints and his unpredictable passes. If he lost the puck the spectators immediately forgave his mistake, so clear was it that his commitment to the game was unconditional. As he followed with his eyes this player whose resolve he admired, Oscar heard, it seems, the central theme of the piece on which he was working, strummed by a dozen angels rocking their bodies like a church choir singing the gospel. There were a few piercing and repetitive chords, evoking the heft of that iron monster with his father on board, hurtling through the night in the midst of a snowstorm.

By the end of the second period, the Habs were so dominant that he lost interest in the game. He got up and left. Outside, the fog had thickened and now assumed the form of a great cloud that lent itself well to nostalgia. He was looking forward to telling his sisters that he'd completed a series of chords for "Night

Train," when he saw, on the other side of the street, that unmistakable silhouette, elegant, topped as always with the perennial fedora masking his eyes, from which there trailed a coil of smoke. *Bloodseed*, how had he been able to find him? Had he passed by his parents'? The impresario crossed the street with a light step, ignoring the cars braking suddenly in his path, their horns blaring. It was a brilliant idea to go and see a hockey game after what had happened, he declared, before shaking Oscar's hand. Brilliant. Was it then that Oscar asked himself for the first time if he would one day have the strength to break with this man? Or did he then accept, remembering his mother's advice, that it was futile to want to free oneself from the devil's clutches? What is certain is that they were seen that same night leaning on the Ritz-Carlton bar, absorbed in, to all appearances, a productive conversation, and that at dawn, on the sidewalk in front of the hotel, Oscar gave Norman a warm embrace, as if he really was sorry to leave him.

6

It's said that, many years later, his hair turning grey, with a solemn air that matched his sagging features and a spasmodic grimace on his lips, Oscar was lying on a chaise longue in the garden of his house on a glorious summer afternoon, dressed in a flat beige cap, linen pants, and a Hawaiian shirt sporting artfully arched green palm trees. In front of him were his young wife, who bore no resemblance to Marguerite, and his daughter, the apple of his eye, who was slowly bouncing up and down in the swimming pool, throwing and catching a beach ball. Everything would suggest that for a second time, Oscar was questioning the very foundations on which he had grounded his life; for the second time he found himself face to face with the fugitive glimmerings of water, not now to ponder drowning himself in despair, but to decide if he would ever again play the piano, since for a year and a half he had performed no concerts. He kept asking himself by what strange detours his life had led him to where he now found himself. How had it managed to rob him of his desire to play?

Wiggling his toes, he saw passing before his eyes, it's said, the dregs of events, the dross of incidents, sometimes of great drama, sometimes of no import, in any case all swept away by the cyclone of time, which seemed to take a malicious pleasure in consuming everything in its path, leaving in its wake only fragments of conversations with no beginning or end, sensations as fleeting as fame, muted sorrows, and hysterical laughter. For several days he'd been setting himself the painful task of taking stock of his life, passing in swift review the houses he'd lived in, the hotel rooms where he'd slept, the women he'd embraced, the records he'd made, from the best to the most banal, the prizes he'd been awarded, the honorary degrees he'd received, the photos he'd allowed his fans, the autographs scribbled in haste, not forgetting the vicious attacks and the looks rife with envy from his fellow musicians.

He remembered that, as his renown reached Himalayan heights, just as Davina had predicted, he swelled up like a pumpkin at the end of autumn, like those found in the lake-strewn region north of Toronto where his country house nestled at the bottom of a small valley. Even before reaching the crest of maturity, because of his precarious balance, he had to walk with a cane, one with a knob of gold that he'd chosen to blend practicality with pleasure. That amused him, because the object in question reminded him of his childhood, when the first ship's captain to sail up the river to port at the end of winter received just such a gift from the authorities. He advanced slowly, as if floating in an aquarium, while his speech began to be punctuated with silences, marked by wisdom, claimed his admirers—tainted by insufferable vanity, replied his detractors.

How many parties did he attend where he installed himself in an armchair and didn't get up for the whole evening? He showed off his designer shirts, his expensive suits, bracelets, chains, and gold rings. When his acquaintances teased him about his taste for luxury, he argued that he had the money and asked, not as a jest, if it was a crime to enjoy what was beautiful. As if to excuse himself, he'd talk to anyone at all with the same naturalness as when he was a novice pianist taking pains to hide the holes in his pants and his threadbare jacket. He was always lavish with his compliments and avoided references to stars unless he was asked a question about one artist in particular, and above all he was self-mocking to a fault, according to some of his detractors: he practised the piano less and less, talent was important but you had to give luck its due, and even if he gave his all every night, you never knew what might happen. If you got out on the wrong side of the bed you could botch everything just like that, he said, snapping his fingers—the spark of genius or run-of-the-mill adequacy, it all depended.

During one of those evenings, Duke E., now a friend, gave him a warm ovation, as much to make a strong impression on the other guests as on Oscar, and remarked: You're pretty as a picture, O.P.! I figure life's treating you well. He looked him up and down from head to toe. Really, you're the maharajah of the piano, my friend! Everyone present had a good laugh, but the nickname stuck like a birthmark, and far from being offended by it, O.P. was delighted.

For his denigrators, he was no longer, in public, just the person he was in private, but also the fictional Oscar portrayed in newspaper profiles. One has to acknowledge that the half-truths, the factual errors, the approximations, and the virtues attributed to him added up to a personage as credible as it was seductive. No doubt he tried to distinguish the true from the false, but it would seem that he couldn't always remember if he'd acquired a certain character trait before or after reading about it in the paper.

If radio loved Oscar, television adored him, and now he was as ubiquitous as those secret agents who were to be found everywhere on his small screen, always in the right place at the right time. Television warmed immediately to his good-natured smiles, his anecdotes that paid homage to jazz legends while teasing them at the same time, his entertaining teaching sessions on the history of jazz piano, and of course his playing, which was never dark and not the least bit hermetic, as was the case with too many jazzmen, in the opinion of one celebrated host and ardent admirer, for whom O.P. was a veritable ray of sunshine beaming into the viewers' living rooms.

He was one of the rare pianists to spurn the bandwagon of bebop; from the very start he found what was "cool" tedious and chuckled to himself when the public tired of its overrated, languorous moods; he listened in when hard bop took off with its eruptions and calculated insolence, only to chortle away when music lovers began to find it not radical enough; he knit his brows before the "free" jazz cacophony, conceding that the idea of total rhythmic and melodic liberty was seductive on paper, but, *bloodseed*, a deadly bore in its application; he laughed up his sleeve when almost all the jazz community began to find those pieces gratuitous, even lazy; he was all ears when jazz fusion made its appearance, he even equipped himself with several synthesizers that he lovingly set up in his recently installed basement studio, but he never, never deigned to give a so-called electric show, since in his head it was clear that these toys were there to distract him from time to time, preferably in private, and not to show the way to an ordained future for jazz, as was asserted by the pretentious Miles D., convert to the religion of electronic music and the mind-numbing beat of rock, the laughable éminence grise who sought the attention of the rock audience, not seeing that this trend was going to render jazz trivial, wrenching it off its foundations of lived experience and authenticity; and when the young Turks started to claim that from now on you had to return to acoustic instruments, Oscar couldn't help but complain to those near to him: All that for this? Ah, *bloodseed*, if only they'd listened to him, he could have spared so many people so many dead ends and such a huge waste of time. It don't mean a thing if it ain't got no swing, he insisted, to clinch his argument.

When he ran into other jazzmen, in a colleague's living room or during a birthday celebration, it's said that he pricked up his ears: contrary to popular belief, they didn't chat about music but cash, about the ever increasing hold of money on the music "industry," since now no one recoiled when you used that word. They complained about the fierce competition of rock'n'roll, and then in later years of just plain rock, while he retorted: But what did you expect, boys? To have a blank cheque for the rest of your days? The truth is that we've had it easy up to now, and I don't know if you're like me, but for me, to put up a good fight—he said, making as if to spit into his palms and roll up the sleeves of his suit—I don't mind that at all. He then repeated one of his mother's favourite sayings—he who knows the other and knows himself can wage a hundred battles without ever being in danger—before people started whispering behind his back that success had really gone to his head. Easy for him to talk like that, they went on, when they were off to the side, he was one of the elite, whose members you could count on the fingers of one hand, who, year in year out, on any continent, filled the most prestigious concert halls in the world, going from ovation to ovation, like the Napoleons of jazz.

Meanwhile, it seemed that Marguerite had overcome her timidity, and her tongue was loosened more and more so that she was arguing over anything at all. He asked her to be quiet, and she in turn reminded him that she had the right to express herself, and he wasn't nine years old any more, playing horseshoes with his friends in the park. From that point on, Oscar lamented to his sisters, this woman used the secrets he'd shared with her to back him against the wall and sap his confidence. She insisted that his hard childhood had made him violent, verbally at least. And it was this woman, whom he'd idealised as a child, whose image had been a beacon for him for so many years, who was unable to appreciate him at his full value? For proof, he cited her disparaging judgments in his regard. They exchanged hurtful remarks that, one by one, dissolved their bonds and made them forget all they had in common, and in the end she retreated to wall herself off in a silence that, for Oscar, confirmed that she'd run out of arguments and was in the wrong.

Many years passed without his setting foot in Montreal, since he'd taken to paying his mother's train ticket so she could come and visit him. He accepted with pleasure the invitation to open a new concert hall, but was shocked to discover that cranes, with a voracious appetite, were gobbling up whole sections of the neighbourhood and that thousands of families had been uprooted on short notice. As his childhood street was situated on the axis leading to the centre of town, it had been selected by the authorities to have built over its head a huge concrete autoroute, along which flowed a constant stream of cars, motorcycles, buses, and trucks. When you had a coffee in the morning, the cups shook as if they were shivering from cold, and when you wanted to talk, no matter the time of day, you had to yell to make yourself heard. In the evening, when you turned on the television set, you would have thought that all the channels had reached a common accord to broadcast only silent films, since you couldn't hear a thing. At night, as the traffic rumbled on without stopping, the whole family dreamed of endless automobile trips. But why didn't you say anything? he asked his mother. If you want to move, you only have to tell me, all right? Davina, whose face was now as wrinkled as an elephant's behind, just murmured: But where on earth do you want me to go? I'm at home here, and no highway is going to drive me out!

When journalists asked him about the winds of change that continued to bear down on Montreal, he claimed to like them, but in conversations with his friends, he showed himself to be heartbroken. It seemed as if someone were amusing himself reshaping his childhood neighbourhood with an eraser in hand, since several families in the West Indian community had finally pulled up stakes after repeated cuts to their water, gas, and electricity on the part of the authorities, and a number of street names had been become French. What's more, monuments to francophone personalities had been erected, and everywhere French was heard, in the businesses as well as in the parks. *Bloodseed*, he was conflicted: on the one hand, he was staggered by the speed with which the francophones had taken themselves in hand; on the other, he envied their progress, especially when he compared their situation to that of his community, still saddled with the worst jobs and the day-to-day racism whose existence everyone tried to deny. Is that when he began to cultivate his love for Canada at the expense of his attachment to his native province? The truth is that most of the time he avoided speaking out on political matters, at least in public. Still, it was during this period that he decided to write an ode to Canada, an entire disc where he praised the beauty of each region, the values that unified this great nation populated by diverse communities, some there for thousands of years, others for centuries, and still others recently arrived from the four corners of the world. When the *Canadiana Suite* was released his admirers called it a masterpiece, so much did his talents as a composer, deployed too rarely up to then, burst forth in broad daylight, as impressive in the ballad as in swing and gospel. The naysayers, unsurprisingly, poked fun at those pieces, which they described as simplistic and full of good intentions that ought not to deceive any music lover worth his salt. When old Jackson was asked about it all, she always replied, between two puffs on her cigar: Leave O.P. alone, okay? He composes for his pleasure, and if his music pleases people, so much the better, and if not, let those who don't like it just change the station, *rawtid*.

During this time, Norman G. lengthened his tours without consulting him, while demanding more and more recordings. Oscar turned out so many records in a year that he sometimes asked himself out loud in an interview if he'd recorded such and such a piece, yes or no, invariably drawing chuckles from his detractors. What is more, his impresario often attributed his success not to the talent of his protégé, but to his own business savvy, after which Oscar, it's said, swore to God that he'd break with Norman, but the next day—a night's sleep counselling, no doubt, some sober second thought,—you saw him having breakfast head to head with his impresario as if nothing had occurred. Wealth lends mediocrity a certain aura, the denigrators said. Why put an end to a collaboration that, though it had its low points, produced good results overall? replied his admirers. Still, as time went on, Oscar often had to choke back his irritation when he didn't choose to make himself scarce if he saw Norman coming. As for that, as if to prove to him that he was dealing with a superior being, Norman would turn up wherever Oscar was hunkering down, whether in the toilets of a quiet café, on a New York square, or on the roof terrace of a hotel.

Meanwhile, Oscar had dissolved his trio with Ray and Herb, despite all it had done to make his name. On the one hand, he'd seemed to have exhausted the trio's possibilities, and on the other, he could no longer go on struggling to make Herb stop drinking, keep an eye on him before every show, wake him in his hotel room in desperation to push him under the shower, or go looking for him on the other side of town where he lay hurt at the bottom of a brothel staircase or, even worse, in the repellent jail of a small-town police station in the American South.

One morning Oscar received a call from Hans Georg B., a sound engineer who had perfected the ultrasensitive microphones used for recording classical music and who had just launched a jazz recording company, whose first offerings featured German musicians. The multimillionaire, whom Oscar knew by name, invited him to his home for an extremely lucrative private concert, an invitation that O.P. accepted with alacrity, perhaps hoping that such an adventure would offer him a needed change. As it turned out, Hans Georg, a short man with a cheerful smile always on his lips, knowledgeable about his work, was able to describe in great detail his favourites among Oscar's recordings, whose slightest nuances inspired, under his scrutiny, reflections on love, life, and death, as if he were analysing a philosophical treatise.

Hans Georg lived in a castle tucked away in the Black Forest, which, with its vast flower garden, its tall towers, and its lush private forest, seemed to have come right out of a fairy tale for children. Oscar and Hans Georg communicated through the latter's eldest daughter, who translated their conversations on the fly. Hans Georg showed him, not without pride, the piano he'd bought especially for the concert, knowing full well that it was his favourite model. With a hand-picked audience of forty, including industrialists, neighbours, and famous artists, the show was a great success, or at least that's what Oscar later claimed, considering it one of his best performances. What is more, spending a weekend with Hans Georg and his wife, who got along so well together, was a great comfort to him, even as it brought home to him the failure of his marriage with Marguerite.

Shortly after completing a recording under Hans Georg's direction, Oscar declared in several interviews that it was the disc of a lifetime, with its bass notes like cannon shots and its trebles like the lapping of a crystalline stream. He took every opportunity to assert that his playing, on that record, had matured, and that his touch had achieved a fine balance between an assured approach and an ironic restraint whose expressive power led him into virgin territory. His music, he concluded, half in jest, had caught fire in the log-fire warmth, in the congenial atmosphere of Hans Georg's castle. Was this a deliberate barb aimed at Norman G. via the media? Was he not afraid of incurring his rancour? Certainly, when asked questions about his impresario, he just answered with his usual smile, glanced at his watch, and claimed to be late for an appointment. It seems that, without any open disagreement, he and Norman had stopped communicating, and from then on, when one learned of the other's presence in a particular place, whether it was a restaurant, a bar, or a festival tent, he quietly left, in full view of people nearby, who only days later realized why he had disappeared so suddenly.

After the Second World War, there began a conflict called the "Cold War," in theory involving no combat on the ground, but only verbal attacks. The United States seemed to have found a good match in the USSR, just as greedy and taken to boasting and to converting the rest of the world to its cause. And so the two showboats transformed the entire world into a chessboard divided between them. The other countries had to follow, from the sidelines, the volleys of abuse they exchanged over the red telephone or risk a dizzying devaluation of their currencies, or even worse, a military occupation—a friendly one, that goes without saying. Fed up with so much vanity and the unquenchable desire for expansion, there were many, like Davina, who talked about two spoiled children who, as soon as they spotted the other child with a toy in his hand, went after him to take it away. As the conflict dragged on, the USSR made Oscar an offer for a series of concerts that was so tempting that he accepted instantly, flattered, it's said, to be honoured with an invitation made only to the greats, delighted with this new project that seemed to come just at the right time, and persuaded that he could achieve two goals at once: realizing a youthful dream of contributing to the reconciliation of the two great powers and coming to terms with his marriage, as Marguerite would be along on the trip.

At the airport, as Oscar later told the story, he and Marguerite were met by a glum, cadaverous bureau-crat who confused him with another famous jazz pia-nist. They were put up in a hotel where there was an agricultural fair, and whose lobby was being used as a warehouse for crates of chickens who eyed them fear-fully and shed feathers faster than the speed of light. Wherever they went, a young man, his skull shaved bare and his skin so flushed that he seemed to be in a perpet-ual state of dread, followed them. Moreover, was it his imagination, or did the people who'd shaken his hand really wipe their own palms immediately afterwards? *Bloodseed,* was he going crazy, or were these things really happening? He'd spent two hours in this country, as frigid as his own, when already he regretted having come, embarrassed by his own naiveté which had had him believe that his music would nourish a friendship between those two giants. Did he then hear Davina's voice echoing inside his head, asking him if, yes or no, he had the brain of an anteater?

He preferred the countryside to the cities, where the audiences were more spontaneous and friendly. Back in the capital, after concerts that took place at unusual hours such as early afternoon or early morning, he and Marguerite took long walks. He was passionate about photography, and so he carried his camera and lenses with him wherever he went, but the man with the pale complexion who followed him around everywhere forbade him to photograph just about anything that piqued his curiosity: a countrywoman in a headscarf who was stirring a pot on the sidewalk, a church square where there was a crowd gathered, young people dressed in T-shirts featuring the image of a popular American singer. Not wanting to provide any ammunition for their mysterious hosts, he and Marguerite kept their composure, at least in public.

It's said that one night, in their room, Oscar suggested that they stop ignoring the obvious: He no longer recognized himself in the image she reflected back to him. She seemed to see him as an angry man, obsessed with his own fame. He wasn't blind, their marriage had been an empty shell for a long time. Marguerite lowered her eyes with a solemn look, but soon raised her head to meet his gaze. When he moved towards her to take her in his arms and head off another argument, she pulled back angrily, and when he persevered, Marguerite's brow and her eyes went black as quick as a city being darkened by clouds. She exclaimed that she'd had enough of being forced to put up with his whims and the temper tantrums of a "great artist," of playing the role of this young girl he idealized above all else, and who paradoxically she could never equal, she was fed up with having to pretend to share all his absurd memories from the hospital. Norman G. had warned her that their rupture was inevitable. When Oscar heard those words, his face went red, but she defied his gaze. What's so sad in all this is you, you don't believe in anything except your music. You don't even believe in God anymore, she snapped. How can you live like that? Oscar stared at her, furious, raised his hand, saw that she was dry-eyed, then turned away and slammed the door behind him.

Back home, she moved to the other side of Toronto so as never to see him again. It's said that for months, after his shows, he led a life that he'd always spurned up to then, going to bars, drinking heavily, and surrounding himself with women who sat on his knees the first chance they got. It seemed that he took to the life of a bohemian jazzman with no trouble at all, surprised to discover that he enjoyed it, so much so that he dated in turn a singer, a waitress, and a nurse, and even fell madly in love with a flight attendant, whom he married and with whom he had a child, only to divorce her a few months later, seeing the huge mistake he'd made. *Rawtid*, that hussy, that no account, made her living by bleeding the rich dry! His blunders soon drove him back to his more orderly way of life.

Meanwhile, he kept wondering how it was that Marguerite had managed to associate with Norman G. for all those years without his knowing anything about it. What did that mean? Was his relationship with Marguerite all the doing of his impresario? Had he engineered their reunion, only to have her break up their marriage to get even for the insult he'd made him swallow with Hans Georg B.? Or was he becoming ever more paranoid? He began to think so, he said to his friends, but most of the time he was persuaded that that's how it all happened. Where and when would Norman G. strike next? Had his sadistic instincts not yet been satisfied, *bloodseed*? During his sleepless nights, he thought of phoning him to excuse himself, just to put his mind at rest—as his mother had advised him, who felt that he should never leave the devil's side—but he always changed his mind, sometimes with the receiver already at his ear.

One night, coming back from a trip to Nova Scotia, where he'd given a solo performance, the train passed through his old neighbourhood. It's said that he was staring at the reflection of his double in the window, already dimmed by time, when he saw, through spirals of blue smoke, children improvising a game of baseball in the middle of the road, while others were hoisting a kite into the night's vastness. He then heard a hoarse voice struggling for breath with each syllable, and instantly recognized the distinctive timbre that had marked his childhood: One last thing, because don't think I can't hear you getting yourself in a state. The voice made a long pause as if to gather its strength, and as if it were going to break off for good, it pronounced, in a tone as wan as the Grim Reaper's face itself: *The time will come when, with elation, you will greet yourself arriving at your own door, in your own mirror, and each will smile at the other's welcome, and say, sit here. Eat. You will love again the stranger who was your self.*

When the train, out of steam, entered the station, he quickly threw on his coat, grabbed his suitcase and cane, and got off, despite his initial intention not to make a stop in Montreal. Coming out of the station, he hailed a taxi. As the vehicle made its way down towards his neighbourhood, despite being happy to see again the old prospects and streets, he apparently didn't recognize very much: where there was once a stretch teeming with jazz clubs, they'd put up soulless condominiums that looked down on the rest of the neighbourhood; a new park, built of concrete, was all desolate darkness; and there was no trace of the ball-playing kids of yesteryear. Had he imagined all that? Leaning back in the rear seat of the taxi, he breathed out slowly, certain that the familiar ritual was about to take place, and that the driver, eyeing him in the rearview mirror, had recognized him. He paid, leaving an extravagant tip—not so much out of generosity as to cut short any exchange— climbed the house stairs while holding onto the stone railing and, when he turned the knob to push open the door, saw Prudence, the phone propped between her ear and her shoulder, happy to see him appear, as it was him she was trying to reach. They embraced for a long time, while he sensed that despite the dense traffic overhead, there was a grave silence muffling the slightest sound. It's said that while still thinking of Norman G. and his deceits, he made his way towards the bedroom and saw her, stretched out on the marriage bed, her matchless profile looking serene, almost smiling. Even dead, she did things her own way. Oscar dragged a chair to the bed and sat down to lay his hands on those of his mother, still warm and astonishingly smooth despite their lines. Gazing down on the beautiful, noble face, he wept all the tears his body held, trembling like a child, realizing too late, it seemed, as he told his sisters, how much this strong woman, captivating and down to earth, meant to him. Just what had she been trying to tell him in her last telepathic message? Although he was seeing him no more, he swore never again to set eyes on Norman G.—a promise he did not keep.

Stretched out on his chaise longue, Oscar caught on the fly the beach ball his daughter had thrown. Over his head, beyond the soughing of the maple leaves, the sky was still just as calm, the air as pure, and the few clouds just as fluffy. The thought then came to him that after his mother's death he had entered the last chapter of his life, one of serenity, but where in time every movement became an ordeal, an experience inconceivable for someone who isn't old.

7

Over the succeeding years, Oscar played in several sorts of groups, accompanied by musicians from all over the world, but no collaboration suited him as much as his duo with a bald and moustachioed guitarist, as close-mouthed and baggy-eyed as an undertaker. It's said that he saw Joe P. both as an alter ego—for he too, thanks to his virtuosity, had mastered his instrument, the electric guitar, through his own efforts—and as his opposite, since his new acolyte was as short as he was tall. Whatever the case, he was the ideal partner, since not only was he not intimidated by Oscar's extravagant inventiveness, but he too was fond of spectacular solos. In fact, O.P. now preferred playing alone on stage, to give free rein to his improvising without having to worry about anyone else. They divided their show into two parts, first performing separately and then, each of the two titans throwing off sparks, crossing swords in tumultuous duos, and taking no prisoners.

In those days Oscar liked coming onstage lean-ing heavily on his cane, his mouth half open, his eyes half-closed, presenting the audience with a picture of extreme fatigue, if not degenerative illness. When they applauded, he responded with a painful grin, lifting his cane in greeting before dragging himself to the piano and taking forever to seat himself. Most often, he began with a childlike melody that he improvised in a playful way, as if it were an exercise to loosen up his fingers. After a few bars, however, his left hand began to bear down, and those in the know, scattered through the hall, applauded to tip off the artist and their neighbours that they'd recognized such-and-such a standard. A few bars later the make-believe posture gave way entirely to frontal attacks resembling the growling of wild animals, the swarming of bees, games of cat and mouse, and the sound of thousands of pigeons in flight, signalling to the public that here a genius was at work. Often, with-out ceasing to play, he'd scan the crowd, seeking in the awestruck eyes of each face signs of astonishment, his having just given the lie to his supposed lethargy. The spectators had the dizzying impression that there were two pianos playing at the same time, rising in their seats in search of another musician on stage—for it's doubt-less true that Oscar, never having recovered from that long-ago blow, sought to reproduce in the public mind the shock he'd had on hearing Art's music for the first time. His playing was a masterly succession of furious descents and chortling returns, culminating, against all expectations, in a sense of renewal and a rejuvenating optimism. After that, as if it had come to expect more miracles, the crowd took it in its stride that in response to this tidal wave of notes there materialized a group of fantastical dancers right out of an artist's sketchbook, who, inspired by Oscar's godlike pianism, swayed their hips on stage to swing- era choreography. When came the moment for the thundering applause, he responded to it with a solemn air, as if to concede that, yes, his unequalled playing, far transcending that of any rival, was deserving of that rapture.

It's said that between concerts, he remained cloistered in his hotel room, spending his peaceful afternoons reading, sleeping, eating, and tinkling at the piano. He had become a legend, to the point where it wasn't uncommon to see people not in the know, spotting him in a hotel lobby, exclaim in admiration, stupefied to discover that he was still alive.

It seems that Oscar's concerns during this period were not of an artistic nature. Apparently, when he paid visits to his now-adult children, he saw that his chronic absences precluded him from sharing in the remembrance of a particular family celebration, in the comprehension of a certain humorous, complicit remark. And at any moment he might meet with a sullen attitude on the part of one of his daughters, or a nasty jibe from one of his sons, making him feel like a stranger in his own family. On the way home, in the solitude of a taxi's back seat, it seemed to him that he was paying dearly for what his work had required of him: going away on tours. In truth, people had short memories: Had they forgotten the efforts he made to spare them a precarious existence? What did they think? That the private schools they attended, the fancy clothes they wore, the good food they relished were paid for by the grace of God, *bloodseed*? He went back to his apartment, not beaten down, but furious, and it took hours for his anger to subside, superseded by the unshakable conviction that for his family he'd been irreplaceable.

He began to take pleasure in solitude, tired of furtive encounters with the opposite sex that led, according to him, either to melodramatic fallings out or simply to dead ends. He sat alone in his spacious dining room with its dark, modern furnishings, from where he could see the Toronto lights that lost themselves in the large bay, and swallowed the rice and red beans that usually accompanied the barbecued chicken he bought at the local supermarket. It seems that one night, steeped in the half-light of youthful reminiscence, he heard himself asking his mother out loud if she'd have the time to make him the ginger cake she'd promised him. When he realized what he'd done, he smiled, not without sorrow. Now, when he heard Davina's voice from the other end of the table, he lifted his head and suppressed a smile: Promises are sacred! All he had to do was to tell her in his thoughts how pleasant it was to hear the timbre of her voice for her to reply: What about my voice? I say what I have to say, that's all. From then on, their dialogues became routine.

It was around this time that a rumour began to circulate: Oscar was in love again. Apparently, the match had been lit at dusk one night, in a restaurant over the water on the edge of a Florida mangrove. While a breeze wafted his way, its fragrance enhanced by the bald cypresses, a brunette decades younger than he was, with high cheekbones and translucent skin, bent over his table to take his order. She was actually the head waiter, but also a great fan, which she confessed from the outset. What was it that charmed our pianist? The impetuosity deep in her eyes? Her flashes of wit? Whatever the case, she left her job to follow him on tour after only three romantic rendezvous. And it was then that Oscar reconnected with the light-hearted verve of his childhood. He replaced his dark suits with summery garb, his costly, drab shirts with Hawaiian designs, and began to wear scarves whose colours evoked blue sky, a blackbird's red wings, and the yellow bananaquit. Was this transformation entirely attributable to Helen, his new flame, now his new wife? Not entirely, because when she told him she was pregnant, it seems that he greeted the news with tears of joy: at last he could take seriously the role of father, which he'd sidestepped up to then. Now he refused to go on tour without his wife and daughter, determined to spend as much time at home as onstage, not so much out of love for those close to him, said the skeptics, but because the demons of old age that attack, as is common knowledge, one's joints and the sacred fire of one's will, prohibited him now from travelling as he used to.

It's said that his one sorrow, during those years, was to see how swiftly time passes when you're perfectly happy. Agreeing to undertake one last tour in Japan, he hoped to say farewell to his many admirers, among his most faithful anywhere in the world. In a burst of enthusiasm, he had the idea of taking this opportunity to reunite, one last time, his trio with Ray and Herb, to which he owed so much. The two musicians, whom he saw frequently, since the first was a close friend and the second had stopped drinking years earlier, were enchanted by the idea, and readily accepted the invitation. Arriving a week in advance, Oscar, Helen, and their daughter spent as much time strolling through the parks made fragrant by cherry blossoms and visiting temples with great incurved roofs as visiting photo shops, where he stocked up on accessories of all sorts.

Despite the advanced age of the three musicians, the shows, in the course of which, as in the old days, they tossed each other the ball like fearless kids, resulted in many moments of grace. The night of the last performance, after the hearty applause that greeted him onstage, Oscar confessed to the audience that it was with a heavy heart that he was leaving the next day this land for which he had such esteem and tenderness. As he spoke those words, imbued with a sincerity that he no longer displayed in public, he glanced around at the crowd as he liked to do, and had the thought, according to his admirers, that he could depart this world in peace, now that he had received in return for his music some of its richest rewards. Just as he embarked on the first piece, he felt a dizziness that seemed to him to be the first signs of a cold. To give himself courage, he turned towards his friends, but the malaise—which, he said, was like a storm against which he had to fight—was now full upon him. Soon a furious blizzard attacked him head-on, veiled his view, and coated the arm and hand playing the bass line with layer upon layer of frigid snow.

The entire left side of his body entered into a deep sleep, buried under ice, conquered by the cold. Out of pride, then perhaps out of the conviction that he was invincible, he decided to let nothing be seen of the struggle he was secretly waging, and to carry on as if everything was normal, and many years later, near death, and not without regret, he wondered if in halting his performance he might have escaped the worst. He came to himself when Ray asked him, wide-eyed, wordless, with a nod of his chin, and just like in the past, if everything was all right, but he was too weak to respond. Ray saw that he had to make do without him for the next piece, and he signalled Herb to play the melody of "Falling in Love with Love," even though it wasn't on the program. It seems that at that very moment, Oscar thought of Norman G., and mustered the strength to seek him out in the crowd. Did he really see him, as he confided to his friends? At the last moment, drawing energy from who knows where, he managed to play the theme of the piece, just with his right hand, like a child at his first piano lesson, his eyes shifting from the keyboard to the man at the back of the hall, with whom he'd signed a pact that had poisoned his life, and who, like a grotesque apparition, or so it appeared, raised his cocktail glass, wishing him health for eternity.

The show over, as applause flooded the hall, Helen rushed towards him and called for an ambulance. At the hospital, lying in bed, just like when he was ill with tuberculosis, Oscar was surrounded by doctors who took turns explaining to Helen in layman's terms what the problem was. Not that the terms were very clear because neither he nor Helen understood very much. They had the strange impression that those gentlemen wanted to keep the diagnostic secret to themselves. We don't know quite how a dispatch spread abroad the news of his stroke, but reactions flooded in, and his friends were left stunned. For some of his denigrators, a deep weariness, caused by decades of collusion with the most diabolical forces in the music industry, had taken possession of the left side of his body to plunge it into a lethargy that would be, if not permanent, at least of long duration. Others spoke rather of the dietary negligence of an elderly man who, they asserted, given his excess weight, had been playing with fire.

The fact remains that on that night, O.P. found himself poised between life and death. Despite his mouth being twisted on the left side and his inability to raise his eyelids, he was to all appearances conscious, ready to die if necessary, tired of fearing the devil, if indeed he had come to fetch him. But when he remembered his daughter—how could he have forgotten her, *rawtid*?— he pulled himself together. Did he not want to be there for the crucial stages in her life? To teach her all he could in order to spare her troubles and worries? And how could he abandon Helen just like that, with no warning? When he thought about his music, he wondered if he'd ever again be able to play the piano, and the idea of that being impossible did not shatter him as much as one might have thought. What was going on in his head? As he was slipping into the world of shades, victim to the charms of eternal sleep, he heard, according to his fans, a familiar and indomitable voice call out to him, as gruff as ever: You're in a pickle now, eh? Davina was grumbling as if she were mulling things over on high, and she said, all in one breath: Just hold your horses and wait until you see how the war's going between the Good Lord's soldiers and the devil's army, because as long as you don't know, you're not even a player in all that. Those words, surprisingly, inspired in him a powerful longing to hang onto life.

Soon afterwards, he was released. He was bedridden for months, in the master bedroom of his new house in the Toronto suburbs, mired in the swamp of a convalescence that seemed less stifling and unjust than one might believe. He wasn't so much angry as immersed in a deep melancholy, propitious to self-reflection. What had he done with his life? What principles governed it? Had he lost his way along the road? When he looked at himself in the mirror, rigged out in a nightshirt and an awkward involuntary grimace that reminded him of Art, it's said that he asked himself, seriously, whether someone somewhere was getting back at him for the intolerable jealousy he'd harboured towards his rival. Settled under the covers, he spent his days reading his daughter stories about girls smarter than their parents, helping to dress her dolls, and, at nightfall, studying the drawings she made of him, seeking there an avenue to the future: as though calling him to order she always drew him at the piano, the keyboard unspooling like toilet paper, with musical notes drifting over his head like stars lighting up the lives of the music lovers she sketched in a few monochrome strokes in the corner of the page, all of them with wide smiles. Then, one morning, he asked to be brought downstairs. He stayed there for a long time studying the studio he'd set up: a grand piano, stacked electric keyboards, mixing boards, amplifiers, guitars, trumpets, and saxophones. Suddenly, this space that he'd seen just a few weeks earlier as his lair, his sanctuary even, seemed inexpressibly vain. Before asking to be taken back upstairs, he told his wife that he'd decided to sell it all, with the single exception of the piano.

Apparently, a year went by without his going back down to the basement. When summer came, he began to install himself on the chaise longue next to the pool, from which he followed his daughter's progress as a swimmer, lulled by the blissful joys of inaction, persuaded that life could go on just that way, serenely.

It's said that, one afternoon, drowsy from the effort it took to digest his food, he saw his wife coming towards him, along with a fairly sturdy elderly man missing his left hand, his hair grey and his back bent. Oscar took off his sunglasses: yes, it was Chester, whom he hadn't seen for ages, *bloodseed*! He was attending a gathering of veterans in Toronto, and he'd decided to pay a visit to his little brother. While Chester talked to him in very simple terms, he had trouble persuading himself that it was really him; he seemed to have shrunk and lost his former combativeness. Even his voice, which once had a forceful resonance, had mutated into a kindly old man's wisp of a voice. They spent the afternoon catching up on old times, stuffing themselves with chicken wings washed down with several glasses of beer, occasionally interrupted by Helen, who, from the swimming pool, tried to stem their penchant for hyperbole. At day's end, when Helen and her daughter had gone in after having kissed them goodnight, Oscar brought out a bottle of rum. In honour of their reunion, they began to down glass after glass, as if they were giving short shrift to old age, so much so that after a time Oscar began to see in Chester signs of his former verve. It's true that life had not been easy for him: once a prominent union leader, he'd experienced a slow but implacable decline, like so many of his fellow travellers, since the virtual disappearance of the manufacturing sector in Montreal. People, Chester argued, couldn't make the proper judgments. All the advances acquired thanks to the unions were now passed over in silence when they were not scoffed at, casualties of a collective amnesia and a deification of the present day. After having lost his job as a docker at the port, and as the unions' influence dwindled, the truth was that he'd lived from hand to mouth, going from one job to another, in the end resigning himself to his fate and living off his meagre pension, his activism long behind him.

When the bottle was empty and the mosquitos had become nasty, it's said that Oscar unfolded his wheelchair and hoisted himself into it with the help of his brother, moving to the back door. Inside, in a large room where toys were scattered about, he took a photo album from the bookcase against the wall. They were instantly drawn to the old sepia pictures of their parents dating from their arrival in Canada, where in Sunday clothes they seemed to be standing at attention, solemn as judges, sometimes in front of a wooden house with a tilting roof, sometimes in a square bordered by perky palm trees and taros with their leaves like elephant ears. You'd think it was an old film! Chester exclaimed. After a long silence during which Oscar turned the album's pages with a child's curiosity, they observed, simultaneously, that neither of them had ever set foot on that island. They looked at each other conspiratorially, burst out laughing, and shook hands. Are you thinking what I'm thinking? asked Oscar. Seeing the hesitant smile on his brother's face, he added: Do you remember what *Mudda* said? Youth is a short mistake, and old age a long regret. Chester smiled with all his bad teeth, and at once they shook on it again in manly fashion.

A week later, they flew off to the capital of the British Virgin Islands. Oscar rented a colonial house that gave on a chalky cliff where the waves came to die a thunderous, misty death. During their strolls through town, dressed in guayaberas, with flat knitted caps on their heads and sunglasses perched on their noses, they made their way along the stone road like two snails, Oscar settled in his wheelchair, Chester equipped with a cane. O.P. was delighted by everything: a popular expression— *Cheese on bread!*—called out by a seller of spiced nuts, the winding path leading to a plantation, the smell of a fresh bunch of coriander heightening a salad, the sea views so beautiful that they could melt a heart of stone, but above all the wonderful performances of the street musicians, which clearly charmed him. Quick-witted, their music was imbued with a vitality he not only recognized, but that he felt he'd carried inside him forever. It was one thing to understand the phenomenon at a distance, but it was another to see with his own eyes that his music was part of an age-old tradition, invested with all the island's sounds, whether they were the products of nature, the living, or the dead. And if this West Indian ingredient was the spice that heightened his music and made it different from that of all other jazz pianists?

One afternoon, after a violent storm that left the ground strewn with brown puddles, it's said that he and Chester hailed a taxi, determined to visit their parents' village. The car forced its way through the dense, stiff foliage, bouncing along the road, with its back wheels sliding in the mud. After paying the driver, they continued on foot, avoiding the puddles. As they walked, the villagers halted their conversations, left coffee cups suspended at their lips, stopped braiding the hair of a young girl, lost interest in a cricket match to gawk at them. Several times they asked their way, and each time they were answered with puzzled amusement, followed by a playful exchange, without their ever being questioned as to what they were looking for, though it was clear that everyone wanted to know. When at last they arrived at the street they were seeking, they were disappointed to find that a church had been built—for a sect that, apparently, had become very popular on the island—right where there their parents' first home once stood. They studied the church for a long time, scrutinizing both its foundations and its simple wooden steeple, as if they were trying to imagine in its place the little house with its roof's two slopes, which appeared in the photos. They made their way laboriously to a drab square whose spectacle of sickly palm trees and battered benches robbed them of their last reserves of enthusiasm.

They approached two old women—one of whom, it's said, was the spitting image of old Jackson—who talked away at them, cigars in their mouths, seated in rocking chairs in the shade of a veranda. Led back in time via the comical anecdotes inseparable from the village's history, they realized that both of them had known Davina! The brothers were filled with joy, but after a moment, it seems that Oscar's face went dark: How could that be possible, given that they themselves were in the autumn of their lives? *Bloodseed*, but how old were these women? When, in the course of an animated exchange, they made reference to the years of colonization as if they'd been there in the first-row seats, he remembered his own thoughts of a few days earlier regarding the long life of the street musicians' songs, and, his hand over his mouth, he understood. Speaking rapidly and in a monotone, they'd remembered Davina, one after the other, as if they'd run into her at the market just the previous day. They'd described her in detail: her proverbial outspokenness, her uprightness, and the advice she offered to one and all even if it was not requested. Oscar's tearful gaze shifted from the inconstant sky to a telephone pole where a red-winged blackbird was perched, darting nervous glances over its shoulder like the local gangsters of his childhood. What was he then thinking? Would he have become a musician had he grown up in this place? Was he, rather, meditating on the West Indian tradition he bore within him, which gave him a new perspective on the innovations in his music?

A taxi brought them back to town. It's said that they spent the afternoon on the beach, their feet in the warm sand, contemplating the drowsy sea overhung by what was now a cloudless horizon. Chester told him how happy he was to see him again, but, if he could be allowed, there was one question he'd been wanting to ask ever since they'd gotten together. Why had he given up the piano? As Oscar remained silent, Chester impressed on him that when you have the good fortune to be guided by a passion, you had to fight for it to the death, *bredda*. Oscar gave his brother a kindly look, and the conversation ended there. Did Chester's words influence him? Did receiving that outpouring of brotherly love make him want to return to his music? It's said that during the rest of the day, he let slip his utensils in a restaurant, called a young saleswoman "sir," almost slid and fell backwards in an open-air market where the ground was strewn with shrimp shells, totally absorbed, it would appear, in monitoring the disputes being waged by the various voices in his head. The vanity proper to all artists, music seen as a sacred fire, the cult of competitiveness, God in heaven, how had he been able to haul around all those antagonistic visions for so long?

Back home, Oscar agreed to undertake, at the urging of his doctor, some floor exercises, with his rehabilitation in view. A short time later, impressed by the degree to which his mobility had improved, he asked to be brought down to the basement, but after several weeks his intimates asked him what he was doing, since no note had been heard. One morning, a childlike phrase wafting up from below, though played with unprecedented and disturbing slowness, drew tears of joy from his wife and stifled cries from his daughter.

After a moment, it was accompanied by a chord that soon, as if bashful, was heard no more. It's said that it took months, or almost a year of relentless work, for him to learn to play again, for that is what he had to do. He tried in every way he could to begin afresh: no longer to play to impress the audience, nor to be the fastest, nor to assert some kind of domination, nor to help the cause of jazz, even less to provide for his needs. Now he seemed to want to play, and that was all.

Musician friends visited, but only those close to him were accorded the privilege of going downstairs, of which only three were allowed to hear him play, and one alone—Ray—to accompany him. A few tried to persuade him to come back onstage, some by buttering him up, others by teasing him about his scruples. For him, there was only one important question: Could he offer people a music of quality? Everyone assured him that his admirers would be enchanted to see him onstage again, and wouldn't care if he didn't play as rapidly as before. For Oscar, that was avoiding the real question, so he told them that he'd think about it, and they understood, not being stupid, that he was saying no, even though it appeared, as Ray confirmed, that he much enjoyed their sessions in his den.

Months passed without his giving any sign of life, until the morning when it was announced in the newspapers that he would appear the following summer at the Montreal Jazz Festival. The day of the concert, he appeared onstage decked out in a tuxedo and sitting in a wheelchair being pushed by a technician. His forced smile and his rueful air didn't fool anyone, everyone could see that the left side of his face no longer obeyed him. When the crowd applauded, he raised his hand as if his ears were being assaulted in order to silence this outburst of sympathy. He slid with some difficulty from the chair to the piano bench, aided by the technician, struggling manfully, to the point where a murmur of fear went through the crowd, uneasy at the idea that the worst might happen: Would this genius, the city's favourite child, tip over backwards, his feet in the air, like a little baby? And there were more murmurs when it was seen that his left hand fell directly down, because it wasn't playing, just hanging at the end of his arm like a foreign body.

The next day, most of the critics tied themselves in knots with accounts in which the allowances they made were interspersed with fine sentiments. How wonderful to see him again onstage, because, even diminished, he remains one of the great figures of jazz! But really, they asked themselves obliquely, usually at the ends of their articles, has the Oscar P. we knew disappeared forever? The one plainspoken critic, who for half a century had been praising him to the skies, had these poignant words: In my worst nightmares, I would not have imagined such a sorry show. It hurts me deeply to have to say this, but the Oscar of today is but a caricature of what he was in happier times. Doubtless, it would have been better for him to stay at home and never again to appear in public.

When such words were repeated timidly to Oscar, he replied that his music had certainly changed, but if the magic no longer worked for others, what could he do, eh? In his opinion, he'd never played better. You really think so, O.P.? asked a friend. But of course! he exclaimed, and his eyes and voice were imbued with a sincerity so noble that one began to believe what he said. And on that note of tongue-in-cheek confidence, happy to have piqued the curiosity of his questioner, he described the reflection of his hands in the varnished dark wood of the piano, where they were transformed into couples dancing with the energy of despair.

It's said that one night that same summer, as much to ward off insomnia as for his own pleasure, he was rehearsing in his basement, lit only by a seven-branch candlestick, when he received a telephone call from Norman G., who began talking to him cheerfully about this and that, as if they'd just seen each other the day before. He'd settled in Switzerland, where life was sweet, and where, he made no secret of it, the taxation of his assets was more advantageous. It was certainly him, and his voice, even weakened, seemed to want to communicate everything at once. Had he become senile? Norman paused to indicate that he wanted to see him again, and his blood froze. Why should Oscar agree to meet once more with this man who had poisoned his life?

A few days later he boarded a plane, accompanied by his wife and child, although once they arrived he decided to visit Norman alone. When he opened the door to his house, they stared at each other for a long time in silence: both in the twilight of their years, each one manoeuvring in a wheelchair. As they chatted in the living room about one thing and another, while a dozen greying heads in oil paintings kept watch over them out of the corners of their eyes, Oscar studied, it's said, Norman's aged face, replete with the nose, eyes, and mouth of an old man, from which there emerged an old man's distinctive voice, and he thought to himself that despite the ravages of time Norman still filled him with horror, the one difference being that, now that he no longer had all his faculties, he could not be silenced and behaved like a condemned man who'd been given a few hours' reprieve. At nightfall, Norman rolled towards the tall doors, followed by Oscar. Beneath a starry sky, on the marble floor of a spacious balcony with wrought iron beams, were distributed dozens of telescopes and a desk, where, it seemed, he scribbled notes. Since retiring from the world of music, that was his new passion, he said. When Oscar reminded him that his father Josué also had a love for astronomy, Norman, one eye at the eyepiece of an instrument, shot back: You never wanted to admit it, but we're made of the same stuff.

The same stuff? asked Oscar. Is that a joke, or what? Norman fixed him with his ancient madman's eyes. In other parts of your life, he said, you were original, but on this point, to be honest, you were like all my other musicians. You had to blacken me to invent for yourself an artistic purity that is just a fiction, an abominable lie. You always demonized me, Oscar, and I guess that must have done you a lot of good for it to have gone on for such a long time. Even if we no longer saw each other, there were people who kept me up to speed on all the nonsense you were saying about me. What do you think?

His eyes focused on the wrought iron as if his animosity was such that he could not resolve to look Oscar in the eyes, Norman went on: Once you were famous you kissed me off, then you avoided me for decades. But let me tell you, you'd have been nothing without me, nothing at all! You know, in the end I got used to taking hits, I got so many, from you and all the other musicians. Oh, it's easy to hold a businessman in contempt, isn't it, while never saying no to money? I mean, no musician I ever knew said no to a payday. Isn't that strange? And what about the artists who live the lives of lords? They deserved their money, I suppose? While me, I'm some sort of swine, the devil incarnate? What hypocrisy!

It's said that Oscar was dying to reply, but dying just as much to follow this twisted logic to its end. At times, Norman rolled himself up to a telescope to peer through an eyepiece, then went to his desk to jot down a calculation before returning to Oscar, so that when he picked up the thread of the conversation, his account of their relationship found echoes in his astonishing famil-iarity with the craters of Mars, the planet which, from what he said, obsessed him.

And was this madman right? thought Oscar. And if he'd been spinning himself yarns his whole life long, convinced that his ex-impresario was responsible for every misfortune that ever befell him? And if, during all those years, he'd been living in the cave of his own mind, on the walls of which were cast his shadow and those of his entourage? All lies! his admirers would say. Oscar gave everyone a chance, but when someone wanted to take advantage of him, he was right to cut him off, *bloodseed*. And then, it was quid pro quo, since each had gotten rich thanks to the other. In the end Oscar cut short Norman's fevered oration to initiate, at least at the start, a true dialogue of the deaf. Despite his opposite's indifference, Oscar argued that if everything were to do over again, he'd handle things in pretty much the same way. He'd still walk a fine line between a jazz that made no compromises and one that was more accessible and would not turn its back on entertainment, because he wasn't stupid, he knew that his artistic decisions broke faith with his past, his youth, during which he'd acquired almost all his musical tastes. But he was certain that he'd find himself a different impresario, one more attuned to his music and less obsessed by financial success. The other remained silent, then burst out laughing and asked him if he was serious. They spent all night talking, bare-knuckled, each spilling his guts, forgetting to eat, their throats raw from scotch.

At dawn, when Norman came around to saying that Davina was an avaricious woman who'd exploited him, a witch disguised as a loving mother, it's said that Oscar threw himself at him like a wild animal. Norman's wheelchair tipped over, throwing his ex-impresario onto his back, and Oscar climbed onto him, straddled him, pressing his thumbs to his unshaven throat. He derided him like the gangsters hanging around on street corners when he was a child: I could kill you easily, no one would know, no one's got your back anymore. Norman, not the least bit frightened, gave a little laugh before answering back: It's not worth it, you idiot. I'm dying, I've got only a few weeks left. According to Norman, a tumour was spreading through him like a spider deploying its long hairy legs. After hesitating for a long time,

Oscar crawled to his wheelchair and turned back once more towards Norman, prone on the ground, a look of malicious pain on his face. Then he left. Some say this story is nonsense, and that Oscar, a peaceful soul if ever there was one, would never have paid him the courtesy of even a snub. Whatever the case, less than a month later Oscar learned from the paper, along with everyone else, that Norman G. had died. According to those near to him, he greeted the news with a shrug of the shoulders and a long silence, during which he stared at the floor without blinking or moving an inch.

It was about this time that he began to set down on paper some thoughts on his life. It's said that at first he undertook the project with no thought of publication, just getting his bearings, but bit by bit he realized that he was writing his autobiography. The more he advanced, the more pleasure he took in spending time again with Brad, seeing once more Marguerite's ghostly features in the hospital, and hearing himself performing his favourite standards alongside Ray and Herb. His pleasure consisted in revisiting those places at his own speed. He scribbled page after page dealing with his strange relationship with his impresario, fascinated by each of their meetings, persuaded that every scene generated more questions than answers, determined to stop himself whenever, against his will, he was distorting the truth to favour an illusory life he'd never led. It appears that a number of questions arose in the course of his writing: Did he want this story spread abroad in the public arena? Was he getting too wrapped up in the project, given that after all he was not a writer? Had he not said everything he had to say in his music? One winter night, he tossed into his fireplace all the chapters where he'd expressed himself with the candour of an adolescent writing a personal diary. As we know, he conserved only his tributes to his family members, to the musicians he admired, to Canada, and to his West Indian roots.

During his last years, despite his precarious health and his obesity, Oscar continued to perform, although rarely, despite the condescending reviews, which he apparently didn't read because he was persuaded that he'd never played better, even if no one else could see it. When he no longer felt up to playing in public, he turned to his piano in the basement, contented, it was said, to see his music vanish like smoke, since it was not recorded. Whatever piece he attacked, a breeze always rose up, he said to anyone who asked, becoming a stiff wind that strengthened bit by bit, transforming itself into a fearsome tempest, which rapidly turned into a cyclone that swept back over all the periods of his life, scattering like toys the seats of Carnegie Hall where his American career began, emptying the canal of all its polluted water while he was contemplating suicide, setting in motion as if they were possessed the sheets between each child's bed during the sun baths in the hospital courtyard, and irrevocably leading him on to those blessed days when he raced home to hear, from the living room doorway, Brad's magic fingers which, assailed by the wind's blasts, played at an ever more reckless speed. But why was he always returning to that moment in time? That's what he asked himself as a light snow fell, two days before Christmas, an hour at the most before he died, knowing that his kidneys were failing just like those of Art T., a coincidence that amused him, only surely not a coincidence at all, and he was obsessed by the following question, according to his detractors: Was this Norman G.'s revenge from beyond the grave? His admirers don't believe that for an instant, and claim on the contrary that a few seconds before leaving this world, he had just enough time to ask if he'd be able to play the piano in the beyond. Oh, he did better than that in the land of the dead, says old Jackson, when people come to quiz her. I say he was able at last to greet himself at the door of his house, and to say welcome, sit, just like his mother had told him so rightly to do long ago, *bloodseed*.

About the Author

Born in Chile, Mauricio Segura grew up in Montreal and studied at Université de Montréal and McGill University. He is a well-known journalist, scriptwriter, and documentary filmmaker. An editor of the literary journal *L'Inconvénient* and a regular contributor to the Montreal public affairs magazine *L'Actualité*, he has taught at Concordia University, McGill University, and Université de Montréal.

Segura is the author of four novels and a study of Western depictions of Latin America. His novels *Black Alley* and *Eucalyptus* were published in English by Biblioasis. *Black Alley* is widely studied in Quebec's junior college system. *Eucalyptus* was named one of Amazon's 100 best books of 2013. The Montreal newspaper *La Presse* chose *Oscar* as one of the 40 best books of 2016.

About the Translator

Donald Winkler's previous translations for the Biblioasis International Translation Series include Mauricio Segura's *Eucalyptus*, Samuel Archibald's Giller-nominated *Arvida*, and Andrée A. Michaud's Giller-longlisted *Boundary: The Last Summer*. A Montreal-based literary translator and documentary filmmaker, he is a three-time winner of the Governor General's Award for French-to-English Translation, most recently in 2013 for Pierre Nepveu's poetry collection *The Major Verbs*.